BEYOND the STARS

Compiled by Sarah Webb

HarperCollins *Children's Books*

FIGHTING WORDS Providing free tutoring in creative writing for students of all ages in Ireland. www.fightingwords.ie

HarperCollins *Children's Books* is a division of HarperCollins*Publishers* Ltd,
77-85 Fulham Palace Road, Hammersmith, London W6 8JB
Fighting Words Ltd. Company Registered Charity CHY 18262

www.harpercollins.co.uk
and
www.fightingwords.ie

1 3 5 7 9 10 8 6 4 2

Beyond the Stars: Twelve Tales of Adventure, Magic and Wonder

ISBN 978-0-00-757846-7

Printed and bound in England by
Clays Ltd, St Ives plc

All profits made from the sale of this book go to *Fighting Words,* a Registered Charity CHY18262.

This book is dedicated to teacher Liz Morris and the children of Griffeen Valley Educate Together School, the very first visitors at *Fighting Words*; and to all the teachers and children who have stepped through its magic doors.

SW

Contents

Introduction

Beyond the Stars is unique.

Why did twenty-three stellar children's writers and illustrators band together to show their love and support for *Fighting Words*, a creative writing centre in the heart of Dublin city?

That's easy. Because, like this book, *Fighting Words* is unique. As Roddy Doyle, the centre's co-founder, says, "It's a big bright room. In an area that needs a big bright room. In a climate that needs a big bright room."

Fighting Words is a remarkable place that provides free tutoring in creative writing to all ages, but most especially to children and teenagers. It gives young writers a voice and helps them to reach their creative potential. And above all, it's fun.

In January 2009 I volunteered at *Fighting*

Words' very first Primary School Workshop. The room was so full of creativity, joy and optimism I thought my heart would burst. With the help of a storyteller, an illustrator and a team of volunteers, each of the children involved wrote their own book. On the back of each book (every young writer was given their own copy to take home – complete with wonderful full-colour illustrations) was a photograph of the child's smiling face and a blank box for them to add their very own writer's biography. Leaving the centre, their faces shone with happiness.

Since that first workshop, I have volunteered at *Fighting Words* whenever I can. I have always left that big bright room inspired, uplifted and with a joyful heart. This book is my thank you to the centre, for creating a haven of the imagination – my love letter to *Fighting Words* if you like. I hope they will allow me to continue to be a small part of the magic for many years to come. A huge thank you must also go to Roddy Doyle and Sean Love for their help with this book.

Beyond the Stars would not exist without

the superstar writers and illustrators behind this collection – all of whom said yes to contributing without hesitation. Yes, Chris Haughton, it was a little like "herding cats" at times, but very cool and lovely cats! Thanks to the team: Roddy Doyle and Steve Simpson; Derek Landy and Alan Clarke; John Boyne and Paul Howard; Judi Curtin and Chris Judge; Eoin Colfer and Marie-Louise Fitzpatrick; Marita Conlon-McKenna and P. J. Lynch; Michael Scott and Chris Haughton; Gordon Snell and Michael Emberley; Celine Kiernan and Tatyana Feeney; Oisín McGann; Siobhán Parkinson and Olwyn Whelan; and finally, Niamh Sharkey, who illustrated our competition-winner Emma Brade's story. Mammoth thanks also to Ruth Alltimes, Mary Byrne and their supernova team at HarperCollins Children's Books for their hard work and support of what is a highly unusual project. And to my wonderful agent, Philippa Milnes-Smith, for her hand-holding and enthusiasm for the book.

As the Irish writer Oscar Wilde once said: "We are all in the gutter, but some of us are looking at the stars." With your wonderful work for this collection, you have all reached for the stars, and

'Beyond'. Together, we have created a glowing universe of space dogs and ice queens, invisible cats and warriors brave.

Now it is up to you, dear reader, to continue the journey. Read the magical stories within these pages and let your imagination fly.

Sarah Webb

To find out more about *Fighting Words* and its work turn to the back of this book.

THE STAR DOGS

RODDY DOYLE

Illustrated by

Steve Simpson

Roddy Doyle has written ten novels, including *Paddy Clarke Ha Ha Ha,* which won the Booker prize in 1993, and *The Commitments*, now a popular West End show. He is the co-founder of Fighting Words. He has written several books for children, the latest of which is called *Brilliant*. He lives in Dublin – which is also brilliant.

Steve Simpson's innovative, award-winning approach to graphic design, typography and illustration is built on fresh thinking, traditional skills and a healthy dose of fun. *Mise agus an Dragún*, written by Patricia Forde and illustrated by Steve, was shortlisted for the CBI Book of the Year Awards in 2013.

Звёздные собаки

Родди Дойл ★ Стив Симпсон

MOSCOW – January, 1951:

It was cold. So cold. But the dog was used to it. The cold was a part of her. But the hunger – she could never get used to that. Although she had always been hungry.

She stood on the street, off the footpath, in the snow. She knew the humans would find it hard to see her – until it was too late. She was white, and very small. She could make herself seem even smaller, and the snow was fresh, new, still falling. The city's dirt hadn't spoilt it yet.

The dog watched the humans. They weren't moving. They stood in a line outside the bakery, waiting for their turn to buy the bread that the dog could smell from where she stood. Like her, the humans were cold. Like her, they were used to it. Unlike her, they were tired, numb, half asleep.

She heard the car before she saw it. It had turned the corner but, still, she couldn't see it until it came out of the falling snow. A black car. (All cars were black.) She made her move. She ran the short distance to the centre of the street, straight into the path of the car. There was a risk. She was the colour of the snow and the driver might not see her. But she was hungry. And she was loud.

She barked.

The driver heard the dog, then saw her. He braked, and the car stopped briefly, then started a sideways skid across the ice.

"Stupid dog!"

The car continued on its slow, unstoppable journey over the ice.

The women queuing outside the bakery turned in time to see the car. They watched as it hit another, parked car. There was no sign of the dog. No one had seen a dog. Some of the women went to help the driver, and the baker, a thin man with long arms, ran out of the shop.

"What happened?"

The dog made her move.

While all human eyes were fixed on the crashed car, she dashed back across the street. Her paws were tough, and moving over the ice was easy. She jumped and, with her teeth, she pulled a parcel from the top of a straw basket. It was a gamble – but she knew immediately that she had chosen well. Her nose told her, and her tongue against the paper bag told her: she had grabbed meat.

She'd been noticed.

"Look!"

"The cheek!"

She had to escape. Her size was useful again. She dashed through legs. Hands tried to grab her, and feet tried to kick. Women slid, and the baker ran back inside to get his gun. The dog was tempted to stop, to devour the meat right there – she was so hungry. But she kept going. She was almost clear.

She didn't see the net, or the man holding the net. She felt it land on her back, and she felt it tangling her feet, her paws. She didn't know what it was. But she did know she'd been caught.

She ate the meat as quickly as she could. She was still eating, snarling, when she was lifted in the net and carried to the cage in the back of the truck.

She had heard dogs howl before – of course she had. All her life she'd heard angry, frightened dogs. But never so many, and never under a low roof.

It was dark in the dog pound. There were no windows. But she could still see the other cages and the dogs. They were fighting against the chains that held them to the walls. Pulling, trying to bite through the iron links. And howling.

She howled too, and pulled. She had been here, locked up, for five days and nights. But she didn't give up. She wouldn't. She wanted to feel the ice under her paws again. She wanted to feel the freezing air, and the snow. She wanted to get back to the streets of the city, her wilderness, her proper life.

She saw the door open before she heard it. The door became a crack of light that got slowly wider, followed by the protests of the rusting hinges.

Followed by the humans.

There were two of them. Two males. One of them she'd seen before, the one who came every day and hit the cage bars with his wooden club before he filled their water bowls. The dog had bitten him the first day, and she'd felt the club on her back.

The other human she hadn't seen before.

She watched them walk slowly between the cages, examining each dog. They walked straight past the bigger dogs and the dark-furred dogs, and stopped in front of a cage that contained a small white-furred dog, like her.

The dog, a female, sat quietly in her cage, the only dog not howling.

"This one," said the stranger.

The man with the club unlocked the cage and took out the white dog. She didn't attack or pull at her chain.

They moved again, the humans. And stopped again, at another white-furred dog.

"And this one," said the stranger.

Again, the man with the club removed the chosen dog from her cage.

Here was her chance, she thought. Here was escape. She fought the urge to howl, and to throw herself at the bars of the cage.

She sat – she made herself sit still.

The two men walked past all of the large dogs. Nearer – they came nearer. *Sit still*, she told herself. *Be still, sit still.*

They stood in front of the dog.

"And this one."

"This one bites," said the man with the wooden club.

The dog stood – and wagged her tail.

"Surely not," said the stranger. "You must be mistaken, comrade."

"As you wish, comrade," said the man with the club.

"She is perfect," said the stranger. "We want the quiet ones."

The cold air felt like food. She stood on the back of the truck as it raced out of the city. The buildings became smaller, and fewer. There were fewer of the billboards and banners that the humans seemed to love – 'Glory to the Workers', 'Together We Go Forward'. Then there were no buildings or banners. They had left the city.

The dog looked back the way the truck had come. The road was long and straight, and she could see the city at its end. Far away, but still there. It stood out, with its own dark cloud hanging above it. She would find her way back easily, when the time came.

For now, she had the air. It went to her

lungs, but also to her stomach. It filled her up and made her feel alive, and alert. There were six other dogs in the cage, but she was the only one standing. The others had tried it but had given up, and surrendered to the shaking of the truck. They lay on the truck bed. They were all white-furred, all very small.

The dog stood over them. She would be the leader.

One of the other dogs looked up at her.

"You look at something?" she said.

The other dog looked away. Good. She didn't want to fight – not now. But she would if she had to. She was tough. Like the other dogs. They had all survived on the city's streets. She would have to be the toughest.

The truck swerved suddenly to the left. The dog almost toppled; she nearly fell on to the others. One of them snarled and snapped. The truck moved over a rough, pot-holed track. Soon she felt the truck slow down, then stop.

She saw a huge grey building, as big as a city building, but alone. It was partly hidden by trees.

The driver climbed out and came round to the back of the truck, and the cage. This was the same male human who had selected the dogs in the pound. She had heard his name. Pavel.

She wagged her tail and she barked.

Pavel opened the cage.

"Come, dogs," he said. "Come, furry comrades. Welcome to the Institute."

He had gathered their seven leashes into one hand, and now he pulled gently. He coaxed them to the edge of the truck bed until they had to jump.

The standing dog went first.

"Good dog."

The others followed. Pavel patted their backs as they gathered around his feet. She stopped herself; she didn't bite his hand. One of the other dogs, however, snapped at the human's wrist. He cried out, shocked.

"Stupid dog!"

He examined his wrist.

"You will not be staying."

He picked up the dog and pushed her, almost threw her, back into the cage. The steel of the lock screeched as he pushed it into place. It was a sound like pain.

Pavel examined his wrist again.

"No blood," he said. "Come, dogs."

He led them across the snow to a large metal door. The dog noticed a sign on the wall, a picture of something flying through a cloud, and she wondered why they'd been brought there.

Pavel pulled open the door, and they were now in a dark, damp corridor. The dogs fought against the leashes. They fought each other. She snapped at a dog who tried to get ahead of her. The other dog yelped and fell back. She was at the front. No other dog tried to pass.

They came to the end of the corridor and Pavel pushed open another metal door. They were now in a much brighter room. There were big windows along the high walls, and sunlight broke through the snow that lay on top of the windows in the ceiling.

And cages. There were cages here too, in the centre of the room, piled neatly on top of each other. There were rows of them, like one of the human buildings in the city. The dog could see that the cages were clean and shining. And empty.

More humans, all of them wearing white coats, came towards the dogs and surrounded them. They got down on their knees and patted the dogs. They laughed and looked excited.

A female white coat – Pavel called her Svetlana – stared into the dog's eyes.

"This one I call Tsygan," she said. "Gypsy."

The dog had never had a name before. She had never belonged to a human, or been inside a human home.

The white coat, Svetlana, held Tsygan's head. Tsygan didn't bite her.

"You have had a tough life, I think," said Svetlana.

Another human, an older one, arrived and, immediately, the others stood and stopped looking excited. Tsygan could tell this new human was the leader.

He spoke to Pavel.

"All female, yes?"

"Female?" said Pavel. "I was not told this, Comrade Gazenko."

"Does no one ever listen?" said Gazenko.

"I am sorry, comrade doctor," said Pavel.

"But why must they be female?" Svetlana asked.

"You will see tomorrow," said Gazenko. "They are all light-furred, yes?"

"Yes, comrade."

"Before you ask why," said Gazenko, "it is because of the cameras. The dark ones cannot be detected. Now, feed and cage them. Selection starts tomorrow morning."

★

Tsygan woke. It was dark. Another dog yelped in her sleep. There was no other noise. The white coats weren't there.

She slept, she woke, she drank water from the bowl in her cage. It was still dark. She slept again.

She woke.

The white coats had arrived. They moved around the room, they sat and examined papers, they stood at machines. There was no laughter. It was not like the day before. Tsygan knew this was an important day, a day to be careful.

The little dog in the cage beside Tsygan whispered.

"Why are we here?"

"I do not know," said Tsygan.

"My name is Dezik," said the little dog.

Tsygan didn't answer her. They heard the older white coat, Gazenko.

"No food until after testing," he said.

"What is testing?" Dezik whispered.

Tsygan looked at her. She was younger than Tsygan, and frightened.

"I do not know," said Tsygan.

Something in her, a feeling, nudged her to say more.

"Do not be frightened, Dezik," she said.

All the dogs were taken from their cages and brought to a corner of the bright room.

Pavel lifted Tsygan. He put her on to a metal basket. Tsygan had seen machines just like this before, in many of the shops in the city. They were used to weigh meat and other food. But why were the white coats weighing Tsygan? She wanted to jump, to bite, to run. But she stayed calm, she sat still.

Gazenko gazed over his glasses at the dial.

"Eight kilos," he announced.

"Good dog," said Pavel, as he lifted Tsygan out.

Tsygan knew she'd passed a test.

Another dog was lifted, and weighed.

"Ten kilos," said Gazenko. "Too heavy."

The dog was taken away.

The little dog, Dezik, was once again beside Tsygan.

"What if I am too heavy?" she whispered.

Tsygan looked at the little dog.

"Dezik," she whispered. "You are smaller than me. Do not worry."

"What if I am too small?"

"Don't worry."

Dezik and other dogs were weighed. No more dogs were taken away.

"This is good?" Dezik asked.

"I think so," Tsygan whispered.

Large bowls of water were placed in front of the dogs and a the white coat stood with each one as they drank and drank until the bowls were empty.

"Now, comrades," said Gazenko. "The time has come to explain the male-female issue."

He pointed at Tsygan.

"This one I like," he said. "Female, yes?"

"Yes, comrade."

"And this one," said Gazenko, pointing at the last remaining male dog, Boris. "Dress them in their suits."

Two of the female white coats dressed Tsygan. She didn't bite or pull away from them. They pulled something, some garment, over her hind legs, and up across her back.

"It is like a nappy," said Svetlana.

The other white coat laughed.

They pulled another garment over her head. She could see nothing for some seconds. A human hand went past her mouth, and she was tempted to snap. But then her head came through a hole and she could see again.

"No helmet, comrade doctor?" said a white coat.

"No," said Gazenko. "The helmets are not yet ready."

There were metal rings attached to the

garment – the suit.

Pavel and Svetlana made Tsygan stand in a metal box. The metal box was like the weighing scales she had sat in earlier, but it was flat. There were hooks on the side of the box and Svetlana attached these to the rings on Tsygan's suit. This worried Tsygan but Svetlana's pats and whispers kept her calm.

"Don't worry, Tsygan," she said. "Good girl."

The male dog, Boris, was also standing in his own metal box.

"Pavel," said Gazenko. "Stand here."

Tsygan watched Pavel move across to the other box and stand in front of Boris.

"Now," said Gazenko. "The dogs are full of water, yes?"

"Yes, comrade doctor."

"Very good," said Gazenko. "Commence vibration."

The boxes started to move. Tsygan could feel the box shifting under her feet. The box made little movements, back and forth, and shook. She almost fell but she put her feet further apart and stayed upright. The movements got faster. Tsygan felt like she was being shaken by rough human hands. Was this testing? she wondered. She didn't like it. But she fought the urge to lie down - and she fought the urge to pee.

"Increase," Gazenko shouted, over the noise of the vibrating boxes. "Faster."

The vibration increased and, almost as bad, so did the noise. Tsygan had to pee; she couldn't stop herself. She looked quickly at the floor of the box – no pee. The pee had been trapped in the suit.

She heard laughter now, and cheerful human screams. She looked quickly across at the other dog, Boris, and saw that his pee had not been trapped. It was shooting up in the air, and Pavel was drenched. He had jumped away from the jet of pee, and he was laughing, like the other white coats, including the leader, Gazenko.

The boxes slowed - and stopped. Tsygan sat, then lay down in the box. She felt sick – but also pleased. *Another test I've passed*, she thought.

"So, Pavel," said Gazenko. "Now you understand why our cosmonauts must be female."

"Yes, comrade doctor."

"All males are disqualified. Agreed?"

"Absolute agreement, comrade doctor."

"A rocket full of dog pee," said Gazenko. "That is not a good idea."

As Pavel and Gazenko spoke, the female white coat, Svetlana, unhooked Tsygan and put her gently on the floor in front of a bowl of water.

Dezik was beside her.

"That is testing?" she asked.

"Yes," Tsygan whispered.

"What is cosmonaut?" Dezik asked.

"I do not know," said Tsygan. "But I think

we will find out soon."

She shook herself, then drank. She yawned, and lay down on the floor. And slept.

On August the 15th, 1951, after eight months of 'testing', Tsygan and Dezik became the first living beings to go into space. Their rocket, which was launched from a space station in Kazakhstan, went to a height of sixty-two miles above the ground. It was a short flight, and the dogs didn't go into orbit.

They survived.

Tsygan never flew again. Dezik did, exactly a week later, and, sadly, she died when the parachute holding her capsule failed to open.

Between 1951 and 1961, many more Russian dogs were sent into space, including the most famous, Laika, who became the first living being to orbit Earth, in November, 1957.

Most of the dogs were found on the streets of Moscow. All of them were very small. All of them were female.

The Hero of Drumree

DEREK LANDY

Illustrated by Alan Clarke

Derek Landy is the author of the number one bestselling Skulduggery Pleasant series. He has won awards. He is not modest. He lives in Dublin.

Alan Clarke is an award-winning illustrator, sculptor and occasional writer. His images conjure worlds that are whimsical, darkly comic, magical, sometimes grotesque, but always beautifully executed. His work has been published and exhibited worldwide. Alan is based in Dublin.

"There may come a day," roared General Tua, "when the legacy of Man falls! When his shields splinter under Fomorian sword! But it will not be this day!"

A roar sounded among the troops, and Tua's horse reared back on two legs, before the general kicked in his heels and galloped up the line.

"When they speak of this day, they will speak of loyalty! Of duty! Of..."

The last word was lost to Corporal Fleece as Tua sped further away, but he was relatively sure it was 'honour'. Tua was big on honour.

Men jostled him from all sides, and despite the cold winter wind, Fleece felt uncomfortably hot. It stank here too. Bathing was not high on the list of requirements for the foot soldiers of the Hibernian Army. Being big, brutish and ugly, however, seemingly *were*, and as such Fleece reckoned himself to be a soldier lacking. He couldn't even see the valley where they were going to be fighting - couldn't even see the Fomorian Army amassed on the other side. Although this was probably a good thing.

General Tua rode back into range.

"Here, on the fields and in the valleys of Drumree, we will send these demons back to the seas where they were spawned! Then they will learn what it means to encroach on the lands of Man! They will..." And off he went again, up the line in the other direction.

Fleece turned his head, got a blast of foul breath and wrinkled his nose. He saw Iron Guts, his best friend in the whole of Hibernia, and tried to squeeze through the throng of men towards him. Failing miserably, he resorted to waving and shouting over the soldiers' heads.

"Iron Guts! Iron Guts! I missed that last bit! What did he say? What did he say after 'encroaching on our lands'?"

Iron Guts looked back, and scowled. "Shut," he said, "up." Then he paused a moment before adding, "You idiot."

Fleece smiled weakly, and did as he was told. He didn't want to antagonise his only friend, the only man in the army who had not yet threatened to kill him. He was sweating beneath his chain mail and his shoulders ached from its weight.

He sighed; he was already exhausted and it wasn't mid-morning yet – the battle hadn't even *started* and he needed a lie-down. This did not bode well for any heroics he might later be required to perform. Not that he was *ever* required to perform any heroics, unlike the men around him with their glorious names. Ranfield the Raging. Wolftooth the Cruel. Iron Guts the Bloody. If anyone would ever be suitably motivated to come up with a name for Fleece, it would probably be something along the lines of Fleece the Thoroughly Unsuited to Battle, or Fleece the Far Too Pretty to Be Hit, or, the most likely option, Fleece the Where the Hell Has He Run Off to Now?

Bravery was not one of his strong points. It wasn't even one of his weak points. The fact of the matter was that bravery just wasn't one of his points. During armed conflict, Fleece liked to pick a little section of the battlefield, somewhere along the edge, and pretend to be dead. He kept some fresh cow's blood in a pouch inside his tunic, and he'd give himself a healthy splatter when he got comfortable. Then, when all the fuss was over, he would miraculously recover, and hurry back to camp with all the other survivors. It was a tricky business, and once or twice he had come close to actually encountering a living enemy, but his luck had held. So far.

He didn't like the turn this day was taking, however. He was jammed right in the middle of ten thousand Hibernian soldiers. When Tua gave the order to advance, he'd have to slip sideways to the edge, which wasn't going to be easy. He looked up, trying to peek over the brutish, ugly, stinking men in front of him, and saw the top of Tua's head as he rode back towards them.

"For freedom!" Tua roared, and Fleece

winced as the troops bellowed, "For Hibernia!" and then, in another bellow, even more animalistic than the first, "For the king!"

Swords were drawn and held aloft and the roaring went on and on. Fleece didn't know how anyone could have drawn their swords when they were this tightly packed in. Leaving his in the sheath by his leg, he instead waved his little knife and shouted a bit. It was all fairly ridiculous. Getting worked up about freedom and Hibernia was one thing, but the king? The king was a fat slug who'd had his golden throne shipped over just so he could sit back in the camp and eat and drink while his loyal subjects fought and died for him. Naturally, Fleece didn't count himself among their number.

"Advance!" General Tua roared, and the troops surged ahead violently.

Fleece was thrown forward, his face squashed against the man in front. Trying to regain his balance, his feet were clipped by the man behind so he had to take tiny quick steps. He got an elbow in the face and howled as he reached out to steady himself. His knife nicked someone as he did so and they cursed at him.

"Sorry!" he called. He could feel his face already starting to swell. He tried to slip sideways, to the edge of the throng, but there were no gaps between the hulking, shouting, grunting soldiers.

Suddenly they were moving faster, jogging, but Fleece's feet were no longer touching the snow-covered ground. He was being carried along with them, held aloft by the huge shoulders squashing in on either side. Now he could see over the heads of the men in front. Now he could see the Fomorians, their green skins covered in armour and leathers and furs, as they sprinted towards them. He started shrieking.

The front line of Hibernian soldiers clashed with the Fomorians and Fleece jerked to a painful halt. He watched as swords cleaved skulls in two. Axes hacked at necks and arms and legs. Spears skewered. Arrows pierced. Knives sliced.

"Let me down!" Fleece screamed, but nobody heard him above the roar of their own insanity.

He struck out in desperation, heaved himself higher. Somehow he managed to clamber over the heads of his comrades-in-arms, terrified, trembling like a leaf on the surface of a fast-flowing and ill-tempered stream. Hands reached up, redirecting him, sending him straight to the front line.

"Wrong way!" he screamed. "Wrong way!"

A spear was pressed into the chest of the man beneath him and Fleece tumbled down. He was kicked and kneed and thrown about by soldiers bizarrely eager to get at the enemy. Through the gaps he could see the Fomorians – one in particular, the biggest he'd ever seen, stood out, his green skin slimy beneath burnished-red armour that was already splattered with human blood. His left foot was missing but that didn't seem to slow him, and his headpiece was magnificent, a helmet carved into horns, a devil's face on the head of a demon. Only one Fomorian wore such a headpiece, Fleece knew. This was Cichol Gricenchos, the Fomorian king.

A Hibernian soldier charged. Gricenchos's sword was a massive thing of shining steel. It knocked the Hibernian's blade from his hand and separated his head from his body in one lazy swipe, cutting through armour and chain mail like it was nothing. Two more Hibernian soldiers went at Gricenchos, and two more were dispatched with similar ease.

A circle of sorts had formed in the midst of the battle, an arena where the Fomorian king took on all comers. Fleece wondered what it felt like for the other demons to know that their leader was with them at times like these. It was probably inspiring. Not like for him and the other Hibernians with their fat slug of a leader back at camp. The only threat he'd pose to an enemy would be if he rolled over them on his way to the chicken.

A heavy wave rippled through the ranks, knocking Fleece to his knees, and then General Tua charged through the crowd on his horse, heading straight at Gricenchos.

The Fomorians screeched, maybe warning their king, maybe protesting at the unfairness of it all, but Gricenchos didn't turn and run. Instead he stepped to one side and brought his sword round with both hands. The horse's head flew, and General Tua was thrown from its saddle, the horse flipping over and landing on top of him. Gricenchos didn't even do him the honour of killing the general himself. He left Tua to the stabbing of the Fomorians, and turned back to the Hibernian soldiers, awaiting his next challenger.

Fleece was sent stumbling out of the crowd. The Fomorian king looked down at him. Beneath the horned headpiece his nose was long and his mouth was wide, filled with sharp black teeth. He was not, even as far as Fomorians went, particularly handsome. Fleece clasped his hands in front of him.

"Please don't kill me," he whimpered.

"Coward!" Iron Guts roared, breaking away from the Hibernian men, swinging his sword for Gricenchos's head.

The Fomorian king moved faster than Fleece would have thought possible for someone his size. Steel clashed and Gricenchos sent Iron Guts stumbling away. He brought his great sword down but this time it was Iron Guts who moved, deflecting the blade with his shield and shifting sideways, as nimble as a dancer, although Fleece would never have said that aloud. He watched the man and the demon go at it, snarling and spitting at each other, swinging savage cuts, feinting and parrying and doing all the things that Fleece had once been shown by his father, but which he had never paid that much attention to. Pity. Such a skill set would have come in very useful today.

Gricenchos battered the shield on Iron Guts's arm, driving him to his knees, showing his back to Fleece and letting him, from his low vantage point, look right up between the scales of his attacker's armour to the green skin beneath.

Something strange and foreign seized Fleece's heart. Courage? Was that what he was feeling? He highly doubted it, but couldn't think what else it could be. This was his chance to turn his life round, to do something heroic and brave and noble. Only on the battlefield, he despaired, would plunging your sword into someone's back be considered noble.

The Fomorian king splintered the shield and Iron Guts, the only friend Fleece had in the whole of Hibernia, fell back. Fleece narrowed his eyes, focused in on the gap in Gricenchos's armour. His hand went for his sword, and clutched stupidly at air. It wasn't in his sheath! Why wasn't it in his sheath? His eyes widened as he remembered. He'd left his sword in his tent.

Gricenchos split Iron Guts's head wide open, roaring as he did so, and kicked the corpse away from him. He turned back to Fleece, who only had his little knife.

Fleece had had that knife since he was a boy. His father had done his best to teach him how to throw it. His younger brothers had learned well enough, but Fleece himself had grown bored of practice after a few weeks and never returned to it. It was fairly basic, though, from what he remembered: hold the tip of the blade, get the balance right, throw with the arm and flick with the wrist, and the blade embeds in the target with a solid *thunk*, he thought. Simple. Basic. The only chance he had left.

Fleece flipped the knife so he was holding the tip, and hurled it at the Fomorian king. It spun through the air between them, miraculously on target, catching Gricenchos just inside the curve of his headpiece. What a throw! It would have been a legendary throw, a throw talked about through the ages, sung about in songs, celebrated as the throw that pushed back the demon hordes, if only it had been the *blade* that had hit Gricenchos between the eyes, and not the handle. As it was, the knife bounced off the demon's face, dropping into the slush and the mud and the snow, and Gricenchos growled.

Fleece scrambled to his feet as Gricenchos stalked forward, his massive hand closing round Fleece's slender neck. He lifted Fleece off the ground. Fleece gasped for air, legs kicking and body twisting. It felt like his head was going to pop off and float away into the air. Bright lights were exploding across his vision and the battle raged all around him but all he could see was

Gricenchos's snarling face.

He dug a hand inside his tunic, grabbing the small pouch he kept in there. He pushed out the stopper with his thumb and flung the cow's blood into the Fomorian king's face. Gricenchos snarled and snapped, but finally had to drop Fleece in order to wipe the blood from his eyes.

As Fleece tried to crawl away, his own side swarmed the area. Someone kicked him as they ran by and he sprawled on to his back, gazing up at the grey sky with the grey clouds drifting across it, bringing the promise of more snow. Then someone else stepped on his face and he gladly sank into unconsciousness.

When he woke, it was snowing and there were hands on him. He kept his eyes closed. The battle still raged, but it sounded further away. In the distance. The hands rifled through his pockets. The breath was foul. The touch was cold. Demon or human, he couldn't tell. He cracked open one eye, then immediately closed it. A Fomorian. One of perhaps half a dozen who were combing the area. A small, scrawny thing. Not soldiers, but scavengers, picking through the dead and dying in search of valuables. He'd let them. He never carried anything of value on to a battlefield anyway. He didn't *own* anything of value.

The Fomorian whispered curses in that strange language of theirs, and abruptly knelt on Fleece's groin. Fleece shot up, howling, and the Fomorian leapt off him with a scream. Like frightened birds, the scavengers took off, leaving Fleece alone with the dead.

Soldiers, both human and demon, lay like freshly cut wheat around him, covered in a light frosting of snow. To the north, the fighting continued. Fleece didn't know who was winning, and found he didn't much care. Such was the cynicism of the battle-hardened warrior, he supposed. For that was what he was now, and no mistake. No more Fleece the Thoroughly Unsuited to Battle - instead, he would be Fleece the Cowardly, Fleece the Craven, or Fleece the One Who Drops to His Knees and Begs His Enemies Not to Kill Him. A proud name to have, to be sure.

He checked his face to see if he had any scars to showcase his deeds, maybe one along his cheekbone to emphasise how sharp they were. But while there was some swelling and bruising, there didn't appear to be anything too dramatic. Well, maybe next time.

He was sore, though. All that pushing and jostling had taken its toll. Still, he'd picked a nice place to lie down. He settled back in the mud, arranged his arms in a suitably splayed pose, turned his head to the side and opened his mouth in a silent, frozen scream. The only good thing about battles in winter was the lack of flies on the bodies. When he'd played dead at battles in the summer, those lazy, bloated flies would buzz at his nose and ears and crawl into his mouth and he'd have to lie there and take it. He didn't miss the flies. He missed the heat, of course. By the gods, it was freezing. If he continued to lie out in the snow like this, he'd catch his death.

He sat up, shivering, and saw a hand raised in the middle of a clump of bodies, its fingers curled. It was a familiar hand. He crawled over to it, grabbed the remains of a Hibernian soldier and grunted as he shoved it away. Beneath, still trapped under the bodies of more of Fleece's countrymen, was the corpse of the Fomorian king.

Fleece looked around, wondering what the procedure was at a time like this. Surely if a king falls, that side automatically loses? But maybe word simply hadn't spread. Maybe the demons were still fighting because no one had told them to stop.

Maybe no one knew that Gricenchos was dead.

A name entered Fleece's mind, and it was not Fleece the Cowardly, or Fleece the Craven, or Fleece the One Who Drops to His Knees and Begs His Enemies Not to Kill Him. It was a new name. It was Fleece the Hero. And then it was Fleece the Demon Killer.

He seized the demon king's headpiece, hands wrapping round the twin horns, and hissed with the effort of removing it. Finally it came free, and Gricenchos's head rolled back. He didn't look so tough now, being dead. Fleece briefly wondered if he should cut off the head, but decided against it. It would take too long, be too much trouble, and be much too disgusting. So he made do with the helmet, dropping it into a sack that had been used to carry arrows, before making his way back to the Hibernian camp. No more skulking around the edges of the battlefield for him, oh no. No more pretending to be dead, stinking of cow's blood and trying not to snore. Corporal Fleece? Try *Captain* Fleece. *Major* Fleece. He grinned. *General* Fleece.

He kept his grin to himself as he reached the camp. He was ignored by everyone, as they rushed around tending to the multitudes of injured men. Messengers scuttled between tents, leapt on to horses or leapt off them. There was a lot of shouting, a lot of screaming, a lot of crying.

Fleece found the biggest tent, its entrance flanked by Royal Guards.

"What do you want?" one of the guards said, barely looking at him.

"They want me in there," Fleece said, smiling with confidence.

His weapons had never been swords and spears, after all. His weapons had always been words. He could cut a man down with insults and build him up with flattery. With words, he could block, parry and riposte, reducing each and every opponent to a quivering, shivering wreck.

"I have important information for the high generals and the king. They said I should just walk in."

Now the guard looked at him, frowning. "Who are you?"

"I'm the Hero of Drumree."

"We're *in* Drumree," said the guard.

"I know," said Fleece. "And that's what they're going to call me. Stand aside."

The guard frowned, and did as he was ordered.

Fleece entered the tent. It was a magnificent place, bigger than his own house and infinitely more luxurious. At its centre was a large table, at which crowded the high generals, stabbing their fingers at a map and arguing loudly among themselves.

Fleece took a moment, absorbing the energy,

figuring out the best way to approach. With all the sharp words and bluster, with all the blame being hurled back and forth, he realised the only way was his favourite way – using huge amounts of baseless confidence.

He strode to the table, gripped the sack by its underside and emptied the headpiece on to the map. It rolled to a stop, and the voices died down. The high generals stared at it, then at Fleece.

High General Cairbre was the first to speak. "That's..."

Fleece nodded. "I took it from the Fomorian king's head myself, after I killed him."

Another high general slapped his hands flat on the table, like he needed support to keep from falling.

"He's dead? Gricenchos is *dead*?"

"Indeed he is, sir."

"That's... That's... Who are you?"

"Corporal Mordha Fleece, of General Tua's

Infantry, at your service."

"Where is Tua?"

"Sadly cut down. He died a hero, a shining beacon of light to those who served under him. It was thanks to his inspiring leadership that I summoned the courage to do what I did. I'd like to recommend him for a medal of some description."

"The Fomorian king is dead," Cairbre muttered, and smiled. "He's dead. We've won!"

"Not yet," a thin-faced high general said. "The Fomorian Army still fights, and we continue to suffer heavy losses. We need something to inspire the troops."

"Something..." Cairbre said, nodding. "Or some*one*."

He looked directly at Fleece, who felt his smile fading.

"The troops need a leader," Cairbre continued, "fighting alongside them. Now that Tua's dead, they need a man to look up to. A man of courage, of fighting spirit. They need a hero."

All the high generals were looking at Fleece now, and he was feeling quite nauseous.

"I'm no hero," he croaked.

Cairbre smiled. "They need their king."

Fleece almost collapsed with relief. "Yes. Yes, I agree. Their king. They need their king fighting alongside them."

Such was the weight of his relief that it took him a moment to wonder about the feasibility of the fat slug engaging in any kind of physical activity that didn't involve eating. And then he realised that the golden throne at the back of the tent was empty, and there was something behind it, lying beneath a gigantic sheet.

Cairbre came over, wrapped an arm round Fleece's shoulders, started to walk him away from the others. "Our brave king died before the battle began," he said in his ear. "Choked to death on a chicken bone. The royal physician tried to force it from his throat, but he could not reach round his royal girth to do so. The king is without heir. We need a hero, someone of noble virtue, to take his place and begin a new legacy."

"You want to make *me* king?"

"Corporal Mordha Fleece, you said your name was? No. How about His Royal Majesty, *King* Mordha?"

Fleece was turned, and Cairbre placed both hands on his shoulders and pushed him down into the throne. A man in priestly vestments hurried over, mumbling words. He put the crown on Fleece's head. It was too big, but nobody seemed to care. And then, like something out of a bad dream, it was over, and everyone was bowing down to him.

"Uh," Fleece said.

Cairbre pulled him from the throne, led him from the tent. There were people fussing all around him, throwing a garb of fresh chain mail over him that was so bright and polished and golden he near blinded everyone he passed. A belt was tied round his waist, and a magnificent sword the length of his leg was hung from it, the tip dragging behind him like an anchor. Cairbre was telling him something about the battle, about tactics, about leading from the front, and the next thing Fleece knew he was stepping on someone's specially stooped back and swinging his leg over a gigantic white horse, fit for a king.

His royal guard went with him, close in on all sides, making it impossible to break away. Together they thundered away from the camp, into the swirling snow, across the fields, down to the north end of the valley, to where the demons were, and the still-raging battle, and the axes and the swords and the dying.

The guard on his right turned to him as they rode, and shouted, "Orders, Your Majesty?"

Fleece stared at him, eyes wide, mouth hanging open. His vaunted words weren't doing him much good here. His tongue, no matter how sharp, would scarcely nick the oily hides of the Fomorians they were charging towards. He tried remembering anything that the high general had said, but his mind remained stubbornly empty. Fleece the Hero. Fleece the King. Fleece the Forgotten. Fleece Who?

"Charge!" he finally shouted, even though they were already charging. It was something to say, he supposed.

The other men took out their swords, held them high and roared. Fleece grabbed his own sword, struggled with it, having to shift in his saddle to get it out of the sheath it was so damned long. He tried holding it aloft but by the gods it was heavy, and it dipped and stabbed the side of the horse next to him, making the horse go down and the guard who had spoken to him flip over and disappear from sight.

"Sorry!" Fleece yelled, but he could see the horse wasn't fatally wounded and at least now there was a gap. He yanked on the reins, veering right. "The rest of you continue on!" he screeched. "I'm going to outflank them!"

He put his head down against the snow and dug in his heels, letting the ridiculous sword fall in order to hold on with both hands. Behind him, the royal guards smashed into the demon horde. He galloped for the trail between the trees.

Fleece the Abdicator. Fleece the Deserter. Sod it. Sod it all. They could call him whatever the hell they liked. He was Fleece the Living, and he was going to stay that way for as long as he bloody well could.

The Brockets Get a Dog

JOHN BOYNE

Illustrated by Paul Howard

John Boyne is the author of several novels for adults and younger readers, including the international bestseller and award-winning *The Boy in the Striped Pyjamas*, which was later adapted into a major motion picture. 'The Brockets Get a Dog' was inspired by his bestselling *The Terrible Thing that Happened to Barnaby Brocket*. John Boyne's novels are published in forty-seven languages. John lives in Dublin.

Paul Howard's charming illustrations have won him acclaim from both the publishing industry and children across the world. He illustrated Allan Ahlberg's *The Bravest Ever Bear*, which won the Blue Peter Book Award. Paul lives in Belfast with his wife, their three children and his 'hairy baby', Tiggy, a Jack Russell terrier who is very fond of sticks.

Despite the terrible weather – wind that blew grown men along the streets, rain that de-permed perms – animals came and went throughout the day at Dr Napangardi's veterinary surgery, and Abigail Crumb, a disorganised girl at the best of times, found it hard to keep track of them all.

She worked there after school every Tuesday, Thursday and all day Saturday, but no matter how hard she tried, she always made mistakes.

When the Mannerings from Lavender Bay came by to pick up their miniature schnauzer, Abigail presented them instead with a walrus cub, who'd been brought in to have his tusks realigned.

When the McDougalls from McDougall Street showed up to collect their Siamese cats, they were not happy to be handed a container filled with gerbils and a large bag of mixed seeds and dry vegetables that Abigail, in a moment of generosity, had decided to offer them at no extra cost.

The customers complained and Abigail got into trouble almost every day.

On this particular afternoon, as she battled her way through the storm to work, she knew that she was going to get a telling-off for forgetting to lock a chimpanzee's cage earlier in the week – she had spent most of the next day cleaning bananas off the walls – and started to work on her defence.

I'm punctual, she thought. *I'm honest. And the animals like me.* She was so intent on thinking up reasons why she shouldn't be fired that she almost collided with a small boy who was walking along in the opposite direction with the weight of the world on his shoulders. He was wearing an old-fashioned pair of pilot's goggles on the top of his head, the sort of leather gloves you only ever see in war movies and he didn't seem to mind the fact that he was getting wetter by the minute. She wanted to ask him why he looked so sad but there was no time and she marched on past him.

"You'll have to pay more attention to what you're doing," said Dr Napangardi when he sat her down at the end of that day. "No one wants to take someone else's pet home."

And Abigail, who had a toucan, a koala bear

and an elephant of her own, knew that this was true. Should one of them fall ill, she wouldn't like him to be cured and simply handed to the first person who happened to walk through the doors. Abigail resolved to do better in future as she didn't want to lose her job.

She needed the money, after all. She was saving up for a houdah.

Arriving home that evening, Abigail was surprised to find a small boy sitting in her living room, the same unhappy-looking chap who she'd met on the street earlier in the day. He was stroking her koala bear, who clung to his arm as if he was a eucalyptus tree, while feeding peanuts to her elephant. The elephant had taken a seated position in the living room, the one room in the house where he knew he was not allowed to be. Abigail's toucan was observing all these developments from her perch with great interest.

"Hello," Abigail said, and the boy turned to look at her, wiping his eyes with the back of his hand. "Is everything all right?"

"Yes, thank you," said the boy.

"I'm Abigail Crumb," said Abigail. "And who might you be?"

"Henry Brocket," said the boy. "I'm a friend of Lucy's. We're in the same class at school."

"Oh," said Abigail. "Poor you. Where is Lucy anyway?"

Henry nodded in the direction of the staircase.

"Awful day, isn't it?" said Abigail.

"Well, it is the middle of winter."

"Still. Awful. You're dressed like a pilot," she added, pointing at his goggles and gloves, which were placed on the seat next to him. "Or you were anyway. Any particular reason?"

"I want to be a pilot when I grow up," explained Henry.

"There's good money in piloting," said

Abigail. "I could do with a little of that myself right now. I'm saving for a houdah."

Henry frowned. "What's a houdah?" he asked.

"If you don't know, you should look it up," said Abigail. "That's what dictionaries are for. Lucy brought you home from school with her, I suppose? Are you expecting to be fed?"

Henry separated a handful of peanuts into two piles, giving one half to the elephant and keeping the other half for himself. (The toucan flew down briefly and stole one, then returned to his perch; the koala bear snoozed through the whole thing.) "No, thank you," he replied. "I'm happy as I am."

"You don't look happy," she said after a pause. "To be honest, you look a bit sad."

"Well, yes," admitted Henry. "I am a bit sad. But I don't need you to cook me anything."

"And a good job too," said Abigail, marching upstairs to her bedroom just as her younger sister, Lucy, marched down.

"There's a boy in our living room," said Abigail. "He's dressed like a pilot."

"I know," said Lucy. "He's my friend Henry."

"He was crying when I came in. Although he pretended that he wasn't."

"He's depressed, that's all," said Lucy. "His dog died."

"Oh," said Abigail, wondering whether she should go back down and make him some macaroni and cheese to make up for it.

"I'm planning on cheering him up by showing him my fossil collection," said Lucy, opening a box that contained nothing more than a collection of stones pulled from the back garden, but Abigail didn't have the heart to point this out. "And I have a book to loan him," she added, holding one up.

"Very good," said Abigail. "Carry on then."

Entering her bedroom, she opened the letter that Dr Napangardi had given her when she was leaving the surgery and looked at it sorrowfully. **FINAL WARNING**, it said across the top in big red letters. Abigail sighed.

She would have to be very careful if she wanted to keep her job. After all, houdahs weren't cheap.

You might be wondering what a houdah is. A couple of months earlier, even Abigail didn't know what a houdah was, but she knew that she wanted one. Back then she didn't call it a houdah, of course. She called it "one of those big seats with a canopy over the top that I can put on the back of my elephant and ride him around Sydney on sunny days." But then her father said "You mean a houdah," and she'd stopped calling it *that* (the first thing) and started calling it *that* (the second thing) instead.

She'd seen one in a shop off Market Street and it cost three hundred dollars and she'd managed to save two hundred and eighty-seven so she wasn't far off.

Downstairs, Lucy showed Henry her fossil collection and Henry had the good manners not to point out that he had rocks exactly like these in his back garden and had even been considering making a rock museum out of them, only his mother had told him that normal people didn't play in the mud like that.

"How long have you had this elephant?" asked Henry, wondering what on earth his mother, Eleanor Brocket, would say if she knew that he was consorting with a family who kept such outlandish pets in the house.

"Oh, since he was a calf," said Lucy. "A circus was visiting Sydney and they left without him. Abigail found him wandering the streets and brought him home."

"Don't your parents mind?" asked Henry.

"Oh no. They're very accommodating people."

"My parents would go mad if I brought an elephant home," said Henry.

"Perhaps they wouldn't notice?" suggested Lucy.

"But they do take up a lot of space."

"Your parents?"

"No, elephants."

"Well, are they observant?" asked Lucy.

"Elephants?"

"No, your parents."

Henry thought about it. "I'm pretty sure they'd see him," he said. He fed some more nuts to the elephant, held out his hand for the toucan, patted the koala bear on the head and popped a few nuts in his mouth. Then he sighed a little as the rain pounded on the window because he was still quite sad.

"Here's a book to cheer you up," said Lucy. "I think you'll like it. It's about a pilot. It might give you some ideas."

Henry looked at the title page. It was called

Biggles in the Baltic. The cover showed an illustration of a pilot seated behind his control panel, swooping down on a boat in the sea.

"I'm sorry about your dog," said Lucy, wanting to pat Henry's hand to console him but worrying that she might go bright red if she did.

"It's all right," said Henry, putting the book in his bag, thinking he might give it a go later. "He was quite an old dog. And he'd lived a good life."

"Will you get another one?"

Henry shrugged. "I want to," he said. "But my parents say that normal people don't just get a new dog to replace a dead one. They say we need to go through a grieving process."

"And how long will that take?"

"At least a year."

"They want you to be sad for a whole year?" asked Lucy in astonishment.

"That's what normal people do, according to them," said Henry.

"Well then," said Abigail and the two children turned round to see the older girl standing there, eavesdropping on their conversation. "Who wants to be normal if that's the case?"

The following Saturday – no longer stormy, but still quite cold and damp – Abigail was in work when the Dimplefords from Bogota Avenue came in with their two dogs, Hound and Distinguished Lady.

"Distinguished Lady is about to bear a litter," announced Mrs Dimpleford in a snooty voice. "She did this once before at home and it was a filthy business. I swore I'd never allow it again so here we are. You can take care of it, I presume?"

"Our rugs are terribly expensive," added Mr Dimpleford. "And we've just had the decking done. We can't have Distinguished Lady creating a mess."

"Call us when she's ready to come home,"

said Mrs Dimpleford, handing Distinguished Lady's lead to Abigail. "Let's say about eight weeks. That will give the puppies a chance to be weaned."

"Eight weeks?" asked Abigail. "That's an awfully long time to leave them here. Will you be visiting every day?"

"I may visit once," said Mrs Dimpleford, who looked doubtful at the idea. "But then again, I may not. I'm terribly busy. Come along, Hound, time to go."

And with that, the Dimplefords turned round and marched directly out of the surgery while Hound nuzzled his lady friend for a few moments, apparently wanting to stay. (Hound was a modern dog. He would have preferred to be present for the birth of his puppies. He was completely paws-on in that respect.)

"Come along, Hound!" roared Mrs Dimpleford once again from outside and this time the poor fellow barked and ran after her, too terrified to disobey.

Distinguished Lady gave a little canine sigh and followed Abigail into the surgery where, over the course of the next few hours, she gave birth to a litter of seven puppies.

Fortunately for the puppies, Dr Napangardi lived on the premises and took good care of them over the weeks that followed as they got used to the curious business of existence. When Mrs Dimpleford finally returned, two months later – having never visited once in the meantime – she stared at them with a disinterested expression. "Well?" she asked. "How many have we got?"

"Seven," said Abigail. "Five boys and two girls."

"Oh, that's good," said Mr Dimpleford, rubbing his hands together. "If we sell the boys for a hundred dollars apiece and keep the girls as breeders, we'll have enough money to buy that new barbecue patio set we wanted. We just had our decking done," he told Abigail once again.

(He was very proud of it.)

"It turned out a treat," said Mrs Dimpleford.

"Aren't you going to keep the puppies together for a while?" asked Abigail. "They're still very reliant on each other."

"Don't be sentimental, girl!" snapped Mrs Dimpleford, hitting her on the head with her umbrella. "Dogs are an investment. Nothing more, nothing less."

Hound barked in displeasure. He wasn't happy with this description of his species and anyway, he was desperate to see Distinguished Lady again. He pulled at his lead in excitement.

"Calm yourself, Hound!" said Mr Dimpleford. "Fetch the puppies, young lady, won't you? We want to get back across the bridge before the traffic builds up."

Abigail went into the consulting room and roused the dogs. She counted them off one by one and to her surprise there were now only six. Four boys and two girls. And Distinguished

Lady, of course.

"Doctor," she said, looking in on Dr Napangardi. "How many puppies did Distinguished Lady give?"

"I'm surprised you would ask that considering how long they've been here," he replied, spinning round and glaring at her. "You're on your **FINAL WARNING**, remember!"

"No, no," said Abigail quickly, scribbling out one number on the chart and changing it for another as she had a vision of her houdah going up in smoke. "I was just making conversation. Nothing to worry about."

The doctor grunted and turned away. "Get them packed up," he said. "We have a family of overweight mice coming in shortly. And a snake who's been off his food for three months. It might make sense if we put them in different rooms."

Abigail did as she was instructed, packing the tiny puppies into a carrying case where they huddled together for warmth and allowed Distinguished Lady to lead the way out to the reception area, where she was cheerfully reunited with Hound. As Abigail closed the door behind her, she noticed the six puppies turning their heads and uttering a weak cry of regret but thought nothing of it as she presented them to their owners.

"I made a slight mistake," she said nervously. "There's only six puppies, not seven. Four boys and two girls."

"So we're a hundred dollars down on the transaction!" cried Mrs Dimpleford. "How disappointing."

Abigail said nothing. She hoped that the Dimplefords wouldn't complain to the doctor as that might be the last straw and she'd be fired for good but thankfully they simply told her what a stupid girl she was and advised her to study harder in her mathematics class as they settled the bill and left.

★

In Bradfield Park, Henry Brocket sat wrapped up in his winter coat, a woolly hat and a scarf, watching the dogs running around as their owners threw balls and Frisbees for them. There were lots of different breeds and lots of different types of owners: men, women, boys and girls, old people and young. This was where he had brought Benson, his now sadly departed dog, every day for a run and being there helped him to remember happier times.

Some of the dogs, recognising him, came over to say hello and stared around, wondering where their old pal Benson was.

"He's gone," Henry told them, shaking his head sadly. "But he was an old dog. And he lived a good life."

The dogs licked his hand and he felt a bit happier, but not very much. He didn't want to go home yet – it seemed so empty there without Benson – and so opened his schoolbag, took out

Biggles in the Baltic, which he'd been meaning to get to for ages, and began to read.

Abigail's final job of the day was to wash the floors of the consulting room, disinfect the surgical instruments and make sure the place was spotlessly clean while Dr Napangardi finished playing Tetris on his computer. She had almost finished when she heard a curious sound coming from behind one of the filing cabinets. She frowned, wondering whether she'd imagined it, but after a moment there it was again. A tiny cry, barely audible at all. She walked over to the cabinet, looked behind it and to her astonishment discovered a small puppy hiding in the corner, looking quite terrified and alone, trembling, his wide eyes filled with nervous tears.

"Oh dear," said Abigail, realising that she had been right all along. There *had* been seven puppies. One of them had simply gone walkabout and got himself lost.

"Yap," yapped the puppy, trotting cautiously towards her, an expression on his face that suggested he was terribly sorry for any trouble he might have caused but he'd really quite like somebody to let him know what was expected of him.

"I'm afraid they're all gone," said Abigail, picking him up and patting his soft fur. The puppy buried his face in her uniform and she rested her neck on the top of his head. *I could call the Dimplefords, I suppose*, she thought. *But if Doctor Napangardi hears about it, that will be the end of my job here. And I want that houdah!*

"Abigail," said Dr Napangardi, marching into the room at that very moment. Abigail quickly stuffed the puppy into the long pockets of her overcoat. "Everything finished in here?"

"Yes, Doctor," said Abigail. "I'm all done."

"Good. And may I say that I was very happy with you today. You had your mind on the job and didn't make any mistakes."

Abigail reached into her pocket, ready to reveal the truth, but then changed her mind. "Thank you, Doctor," she said, stepping away. "Can I go home now?"

Abigail made her way along the road towards Kirribilli, wondering what on earth she was going to do with the puppy in her pocket. She couldn't bring him home, that was for sure. Although her elephant, toucan and koala bear got along tremendously well with each other she had once tried to introduce a dog to the family, hoping to expand her menagerie from three to four, and the animals had been firmly opposed to the idea. The koala bear had spat eucalyptus oil at the dog. The toucan had tried to poke out his eyes. And the elephant had rolled him in his trunk, then lowered him up and down, up and down, over and over until the dog became so dizzy that, upon his release, he had run outside and refused to come back in. In the end, she had been forced to give him away to her Aunt Jackie who lived in Melbourne.

As she passed Bradfield Park, Abigail decided to rest for a few minutes and have a think. She spotted an empty seat next to a little boy who was reading a book and sat down, glancing at him for a moment before realising that she recognised him.

"Oh, it's you," she said, and the boy jumped, almost dropping the book from his hands in surprise. "It's Harry Breckitt, isn't it?"

"Henry Brocket," said Henry. "And you're Lucy's sister."

"That's right. What are you reading?"

Henry turned the cover of the book to show her. "Oh yes," she said. "Lucy's book. I was sorry to hear about your dog," she added after a moment. "Do you miss him?"

"A lot," said Henry. "He was a *Good Boy*." He said those last two words with particular force.

"I'm sure he was. Will you get another?"

"Someday," said Henry. "If I can persuade my parents. My sister is working on them right now. I'm supposed to be home by the time she goes for her swimming lesson to take up the evening shift. Relentless nagging. That's what Melanie and I are determined upon."

"But they must like dogs," said Abigail. "If you had one before, I mean."

"Benson just arrived one day," explained Henry. "Wandered in off the street and behaved so well that they couldn't let him go. They used to tell me that's how I had come to live with them too," he added, frowning, as if this was a joke that he didn't think was particularly funny. "They said they just got used to me and let me stay."

"They sound like charming people," said Abigail, shaking her head. "Oh, look over there!" She pointed to a place in the distance, somewhere in the general direction of Cremorne Point.

"What?" asked Henry, narrowing his eyes as he turned his head.

"Look! Can't you see it?"

"I don't see anything," he said, turning back and staring at Abigail.

"I must have been mistaken," she said, shrugging her shoulders. "I thought I saw a shark."

"Not this close to shore!"

"No, my mistake."

Henry frowned, checked his watch and picked up his schoolbag, holding on to his book all the time. "I better be going home," he said.

"Goodbye, Henry," said Abigail, smiling at him. "I hope you'll all be very happy together."

Henry walked on, not having any idea what she could possibly mean by that, but as he strolled along he couldn't help but think that his bag was a little heavier than it had been earlier.

And it seemed to be trembling a little too.

"Henry, please don't throw your things on the kitchen floor," said Eleanor Brocket with an exasperated sigh.

"Normal people put their schoolbags in their bedrooms," said Alistair, Henry's father, just as Melanie came in with her swimming bag.

"All ready then?" asked Eleanor.

"Yes," said Melanie, turning to her brother. "Your turn," she said.

"Can we get a new dog?" asked Henry immediately, turning to both his parents.

"No," said Alistair, shaking his head.

"Can we get a new dog?" repeated Henry.

"It's too soon," said Eleanor, reaching for her car keys.

Henry said nothing for a moment, then looked up at them both as if he had just had a tremendous idea.

"Can we get a new dog?" he asked and this time both his parents opened their mouths to tell him to be quiet but before they could a yapping sound came from the floor and they all looked down at their feet in astonishment. But there didn't seem to be anything there.

"Did you hear that?" asked Eleanor.

"It sounded like a yap," said Alistair.

"It did sound like a yap," agreed Melanie.

A moment later, Henry's schoolbag started to move and Eleanor screamed in surprise.

"That's not normal," said Alistair, looking across at his son. "Schoolbags don't move of their own accord. What have you got in there anyway?"

"Just my books," said Henry. "And half an old sandwich. And a catapult. And a collection of football cards. And a whistle. And a packet of ready-cooked sausages. And a novel I'm working on in my spare time. And an extra pair of socks in case I lose the ones I'm wearing. And a false eye. But that's all. Nothing out of the ordinary."

The family stared at the bag and it continued to move and yap until finally Melanie, who was a brave little thing, reached down, pulled open the straps and a puppy bounced out and stared up at them all, wagging its tail as if to suggest that this had been a great game but he was tired of being locked up like that. The family said nothing and the puppy sprinted to the back door, ran outside to conduct a piece of private business before coming back inside and wagging its tail again in delight.

Mission Accomplished, it seemed to be saying. He'd obviously been trained well during his stay at Dr Napangardi's surgery.

"Well it has manners anyway," said Eleanor, who hated cleaning up after dogs.

"And he's a cheerful little fellow," said Alistair. "But Henry," he added, turning round. "What's he doing here? What breed is he?"

"Indeterminate."

"And his parentage?"

"Unknown."

"He doesn't have a collar," said Alistair. "So he can't belong to anyone. And he's no more than about eight weeks old. It's really not a normal thing to discover puppies in your schoolbag, you know."

"No," said Henry, whose confusion right now was only slightly less obvious than his delight. "I don't know how to explain it. But can we keep him?"

"I suppose we better," said Eleanor with a sigh. "We can't just throw him out on to the street, after all."

"But what's his name?" asked Melanie, and the entire family turned to look at Henry as if he would surely know the answer to that question at least.

Henry thought about it. It wasn't easy to think of names just like that. He took his pilot's goggles off his head, placed them on the table next to *Biggles in the Baltic*, and when his eyes fell on the cover, he smiled.

"Captain W.E. Johns," he announced, reading the author's name from the book jacket. "His name is Captain W.E. Johns."

And as he said this, the little puppy wagged his tail again and barked, a tiny bark this time, something to suggest that he was happy to accept this name as his own.

The little puppy had found a home.

For now, at least.

★

To find out what happens to Captain W.E. Johns in the years that follow, read John Boyne's novel THE TERRIBLE THING THAT HAPPENED TO BARNABY BROCKET.

HOW TO HELP YOUR GRANDDA

JUDI CURTIN

Illustrated by Chris Judge

Judi Curtin is the bestselling author of three series of books for children – Alice and Megan, The Eva series, and Friends Forever. Judi was a teacher for many years but now writes full time. When she's not writing, she makes things and takes good care of her tomato plants. She lives in Limerick with her family.

Chris Judge is an illustrator and children's picture book maker based in Dublin. His first picture book, *The Lonely Beast*, won the Irish Children's Book of the Year. His latest picture book is *TiN* and he also illustrated Roddy Doyle's book for younger readers, *Brilliant*.

Dear Mr Lee,

I hope you are well.

I guess you're wondering why a total stranger is writing to you. It's not my idea – I promise. You can blame it all on Mr Jordan. He's my teacher, and he has the weirdest ideas. Last week he

made us all sit on the floor in a big circle. He said we had to be really quiet for five minutes, and become aware of our heartbeats. Five minutes is a long time, and I was mostly aware that Lulu Grimes, who was sitting next to me, has huge lumpy warts all over her right hand. (If you ever get to meet Lulu Grimes, be sure not to shake her hand – warts are very contagious and totally gross.)

Anyway, this week Mr Jordan said everyone has to write a letter to someone they admire. We should tell them a bit about ourselves, and then say why we admire them. Like I said, weeeeiiird!

Most of the boys in my class decided to write to soccer players or scary rap singers. The girls picked cute kids from boy bands, and writers of soppy books about ponies. Darragh Joyce wrote to a fortune-cookie writer. (Darragh is nearly as weird as Mr Jordan, and that's saying something, trust me.)

Anyway, today you got lucky, and I chose you.

Mr Lee, I admire you because…

Actually, I can't finish that sentence, and I can't erase it because we're not allowed to have correction fluid in class. The thing is, I don't really like telling lies. It's not that I'm especially honest or anything, it's just that I'm not a very good liar and I'm always afraid of being found out. So, the truth is, Mr Lee, I don't admire you at all. To be honest, I never even heard of you until twenty minutes ago, when I found you in an internet search. According to the local newspaper, you're the richest man in the city, and while that's not enough to make me admire you (I'm not a shallow person who's impressed by that kind of stuff), it does mean that maybe you could do me a favour.

The person I really admire most in the world is my Grandda. (If you're wondering why I'm not writing this letter to him, it's because he'd laugh and call me soft.) Grandda is eighty-nine and a half, and he's great. He's not cool or anything, but he kind of looks out for me, and defends me when my mum and dad are picking on me for nothing (which they do a lot). That's why I have to look out for Grandda too.

Anyway, the problem is, winter is a really hard time for Grandda because his house is always freezing cold. There isn't any central heating and he hasn't got much money to buy coal. Usually when I visit Grandda, he and his dog Psycho are huddled over a tiny fire made out of about three lumps of coal and a few sticks. I've sat next to scented candles that give more heat.

So, Mr Lee, I was thinking, since you're so rich and everything, maybe you could help Grandda. Do you think you could put some heating into his house for him? Luckily, you own heaps of hardware stores – that's another reason I picked you. It wouldn't cost you a whole lot, since you could just get the radiators and pipes and stuff for nothing from one of your own shops. Maybe some of your workers could do the job in their lunch breaks or something?

I'd be really grateful, and Grandda would be

too – even though he'd never say it – he's too proud to admit that he needs help.

What do you think?

Yours sincerely

Lorcan Browne

27 The Avenue
High Street
Town

Dear Lorcan,

Thank you for your lovely letter.

I appreciate the fact that you didn't lie about admiring me. (Since I became rich, people have been queuing up to tell me lies.)

I'm sorry to hear about your grandfather's woes, but I suspect you haven't discussed this with your parents, and they might be upset to hear that you are asking me for help. Maybe they are busy and haven't noticed exactly how cold your grandfather's house is? If you discuss it with them, I'm sure they'll manage to help him somehow.

With best regards,

John Lee

Dear Mr Lee,

Thank you for your prompt reply. I was the first in the class to get a letter back – I guess the rappers and the footballers and fortune-cookie writers are kind of busy with their own stuff.

I don't mean to be rude or anything, but do you really think I'd be asking a total stranger for help, if my own mum and dad could just write a cheque and make everything all right???

Mum and Dad both lost their jobs this year, and things in our house have been kind of rough since then. (Lately we all have to share a teabag in the morning. I'm usually the last one up, and trust me, on the third go, a teabag isn't up to much.)

Dad says things will pick up soon, and that we'll be OK in the end. That's good news for us, but while we're waiting, poor Grandda and Psycho are freezing, and we can't afford to help them.

It's up to you, I'm afraid.

Yours sincerely,
Lorcan Browne

27 The Avenue
High Street
Town

Dear Lorcan,

I am sorry to hear that things in your family are so bad. I can sympathise because business in my hardware stores dropped by 3.2 per cent last year.

I'm afraid I won't be able to install central heating in your grandfather's house. You see, my firm already contributes to a foundation that helps local charities. I'm not in a position to divert any of those funds, as this would simply be depriving other poor people of help, and I'm sure your grandfather wouldn't like that.

With best regards,

John Lee

Dear Mr Lee,

I asked my mum about charitable foundations. She said they are usually a dodgy tax scam. She said another word before the word dodgy, but it was rude, so I'm not going to write it here. (Mr Jordan doesn't read all our letters, but he does spot checks, and I could get in a lot of trouble.)

You needn't worry about diverting funds from other poor people. Grandda wouldn't care about that. He says that at his age he's entitled to be selfish.

Maybe you could reconsider your decision?

Yours sincerely,
Lorcan Browne

27 The Avenue
High Street
Town

Dear Lorcan,

I'm afraid diverting funds from a charitable foundation isn't a simple thing to do. These things have to be planned months in advance, and even if I started today, by the time things were organised, the winter would be over.

Has your grandfather tried talking to the local council about installing central heating? I believe they have quite generous grants these days.

Yours sincerely,

John Lee

Dear Mr Lee,

Thank you for your suggestion about the local council. That would have been a very good idea, except that Grandda is at war with the council. He set Psycho on one of their workers a few years back, and it didn't turn out well. Psycho is only a terrier, and most of his teeth have fallen out from old age, but Grandda says he punches above his weight when it comes to scaring away unwanted visitors.

So basically, the council won't help. We are relying on you.

Yours sincerely,
Lorcan Browne

27 The Avenue
High Street
Town

Dear Lorcan,

I am very sorry to hear about your grandfather's issues with the council. Sometimes people get a bit offended when they are chased by mad old dogs, even when they are practically toothless.

Maybe if your grandfather changes his lifestyle, he could survive without central heating? On the internet there are lots of helpful tips about how elderly people can stay warm in their houses during the cold weather.

Yours sincerely,

John Lee

Dear Mr Lee,

Have you been paying any attention to my letters at all? My grandda is eighty-nine and a half years old!

He still calls the radio the wireless. When he rings my auntie in America, he shouts extra loud because she's so far away. When he talks about his laptop, he means the dented old tray he eats his dinner off in the evening.

He is never, ever, ever, ever going to use the internet.

Yours very sincerely and fairly angrily,
Lorcan Browne

27 The Avenue
High Street
Town

Dear Lorcan,

I am not an idiot. I thought that perhaps you could look things up on the internet for your grandfather, and tell him what you find there. Then you could take a break from writing annoying letters to people you've never met, and don't even admire.

Yours,

John Lee

Dear Mr Lee,

Sorry if I was a bit out of order in my last letter. I was extra worried about Grandda. He says the forecast is for very cold weather over the next few weeks. (Grandda loves the weather forecast, even though he hasn't been outside for about six months.)

I really appreciate your prompt replies. Two of the girlie writers have sent letters, and one of the footballers sent a signed photograph. The fortune-cookie writer sent Darragh a signed fortune-cookie paper saying 'a blue-haired alien will be coming for you shortly'. Darragh spent the rest of the morning watching out the window, looking really scared. No one else has had anything. With five letters, I'm well ahead of everyone else. I might even get a gold star at the end of the term. (I've never got a gold star before. Mr Jordan says I don't respect authority. Not sure what he'd know about that. I saw him driving and texting last week, and once he made a face at the principal behind her back.)

Anyway, what about the central heating?

Yours sincerely,
Lorcan Browne

27 The Avenue
High Street
Town

Dear Lorcan,

That's OK about your second-last letter. Clearly you love your grandfather a lot. He's a lucky man.

Maybe he could try wearing an extra jumper around the house?

Yours sincerely,

John Lee

Dear Mr Lee,

Thanks for the suggestion about the extra jumper. It's a good idea, but Grandda already wears heaps of clothes around the house. In the evenings, he wears a hat and gloves and a scarf and three vests and two jumpers and a fleece and a dressing gown and an anorak. He looks more like he's going on a skiing holiday than just upstairs to bed.

This problem is bigger than a few extra jumpers.

Yours sincerely,

Lorcan Browne

27 The Avenue
High Street
Town

Dear Lorcan,

Thank you for your letter.

I don't usually do things like this, but since you are so persistent, I am going to make an exception. I am enclosing some vouchers that you can give to your grandfather. With these, he can take advantage of our special offer, which will allow him to buy three bags of coal for the price of two.

I trust this will help him.

Yours sincerely,

John Lee

Dear Mr Lee,

Thank you for the special offer coal vouchers. I looked on the internet and I see that your shops don't deliver. That's a bit of a problem for Grandda. How is he expected to carry three bags of coal? (Have I mentioned that he's eighty-nine and a half?) He hasn't driven since he got put off the road for dangerous driving about ten years ago. (He drove his car into a river at the back of his house.) You can still see the roof of his car in the summer when the water is low. It's kind of cool. My friends and I throw stones at it sometimes.

Mum and Dad can't pick up the coal either, because our car was repossessed a few months ago.

I'm returning your vouchers. Maybe you can

give them to your charitable foundation?

Trust me, I've thought about this a lot and the only solution for my grandda is for you to put central heating in his house.

I await your answer with great respect and hope.

Lorcan Browne

27 THE AVENUE
HIGH STREET
TOWN

Dear Lorcan,

I'm sorry to hear that the vouchers weren't any use to your grandfather. I'll make sure they go to a good cause.

Eighty-nine and a half is quite old. Maybe it's time for your grandfather to live somewhere else? Has anyone ever suggested that he move in with your family? Since the two of you are such good pals, it might work out well. (And he could stand up for you all the time.)

Just a thought.

All best regards,

John Lee

Dear Mr Lee,

Have you ever seen a grown man cry?

I have and it's not nice. It happened at the start of the winter, when Mum tried to persuade Grandda to come and stay with us for a while.

"I'm not leaving my house," he said. "When the time comes, they'll take me out of here in a box."

I thought he meant a horse box or something, because Grandda always likes watching horse races on the TV. Mum told me later that he meant a coffin, and that made me cry a bit too when no one was looking.

Please, Mr Lee, you've got to do something.

Yours in desperation,

Lorcan Browne

27 The Avenue
High Street
Town

Dear Lorcan,

You're not going to leave me alone, are you?

John Lee

Dear Mr Lee,

No.

Lorcan Browne

27 The Avenue
High Street
Town

Dear Lorcan,

I surrender. Please send me your grandfather's address, and tell him I will visit him later this week. Please arrange for your parents to be there too. I might need someone to stand between me and Psycho.

Yours sincerely,

John Lee

Dear Mr Lee,

Thank you very, very, very, very much. Grandda lives at 27 Forest Lane. I've told him you're not from the council, but just in case he forgets and sets Psycho on you, maybe you should have a few doggy treats in your pocket. His favourites are the rabbit-flavoured ones that come in a blue bag.

Yours in gratitude,
Lorcan Browne

27 The Avenue
High Street
Town

Dear Lorcan,

Please tell your grandfather I will be there on Friday at 12 o'clock. I will bring a big sack of treats for Psycho. (Luckily we sell them in the hardware store.) We're all out of rabbit-flavoured ones, so let's hope he likes turkey too.

Yours,

John Lee

Dear Mr Lee,

Thanks for visiting Grandda. I asked him if you were nice, and he said you weren't too bad. That's a big deal, because Grandda hates everyone except for me and my mum and dad. (And I think he might even hate my dad a small little bit. He still thinks Mum should have married the guy who runs the fish and chip shop.)

Psycho really enjoyed the turkey-flavoured treats. He managed to tear the bag open, and he ate them all on Friday night while Grandda was in bed.

In case you're ever wondering, doggy vomit really stinks!

Yours sincerely,

Lorcan

27 The Avenue
High Street
Town

Dear Lorcan,

Your grandda isn't too bad either. The story he told me about the council man was very funny. I hope he was exaggerating.

Your mum and dad aren't too bad either. I presume you know that your mother is a genius? She managed to fix my smartphone, which has been acting up for weeks. There's a vacancy in the computer department of my firm, and if she's interested, tell her to get in touch. You know my address!

Yours truly,

John

PS You were right about your grandfather's house. It was completely freezing, and I am embarrassed that I didn't act sooner.

Dear Mr Lee,

Don't be embarrassed. None of this is your fault, and now you're being super-nice, which is always good.

Mum thought you might have been kidding about the job, but she was desperate, so that's why she decided to take a chance and call you. She's going to start next week, but you know that, don't you?

I didn't like to distract you from Grandda's heating problems, but things weren't great in our place lately either. Now, with Mum working, I might get a teabag all to myself at breakfast time. I'm looking forward to that.

Thank you very, very much.

Lorcan

27 The Avenue
High Street
Town

Dear Lorcan,

You are most welcome.

Please tell your grandda that the work on his heating will start on Tuesday. The men have already packed up the spare van with tools and pipes and radiators and rabbit-flavoured doggy treats.

Yours truly,

John Lee

Dear Mr Lee,

I've just got back from Grandda's place. The heating is already working, and he says you're going to pay for all the heating oil he needs. That's super generous of you. Grandda's house was baking hot and we all had to sit in our T-shirts. Psycho was sweating like a pig.

Thank you so, so, so, so much.
Lorcan Browne

27 The Avenue
High Street
Town

Dear Lorcan,

You are most welcome. It has been a pleasure dealing with your family. Your parents are fine people, your grandfather is an… interesting man, and Psycho isn't all that scary – once you get to know him.

I am glad everything has been sorted out. I confess I will miss your letters.

Yours,

John

Dear John,

My teacher, Mr Jordan, has asked everyone in our class to write a letter to someone they admire, and I chose you.

I admire you because you are kind and funny and thoughtful and you have changed my family's life for ever.

Love from your very good friend,

Lorcan

A Winter's Tale: The Lookout

EOIN COLFER

Illustrated by
Marie-Louise Fitzpatrick

Eoin Colfer is best known for the Artemis Fowl series, which has topped the bestseller lists around the world and won numerous awards. He has also written the WARP series and the Legends series for younger readers, as well as crime books for adults. He lives in Wexford, Ireland, with his wife Jackie, his sons Finn and Seán and an overactive imagination. Eoin is currently the Irish Children's Laureate, Laureate na nÓg.

Marie-Louise Fitzpatrick is an author and illustrator. Her publications include the picture books *There*, *The Sleeping Giant*, *I'm a Tiger Too!* and *I Am I*, and the novels *Timecatcher*, *Dark Warning* and *Hagwitch*. Her work has won the CBI Book of the Year Award four times. Marie-Louise lives in County Wicklow, Ireland.

I am writing this down because Dick is such a pain in the neck. Everything has to be his way or go back to where you came from. He would break the sky if he could, and throw back the waves from the black rocks below our hut. He is what we call stubborn as a bent nail,

with a look in his eyes that would scare cows. And cows are generally too stupid to be scared even on their way to the slaughterhouse. Dick says write it down. So I am.

Americans love the poor Irish bit, says Dick. And your pathetic story has all the ingredients for a Hollywood movie. An orphan farmed out to a crazy old man. Gold dust. Also when you are occupied scribbling in that notebook I can listen to *The Archers* in peace.

Not that I am an orphan, technically. But my father *is* gone, and my mother might as well be, for all the good she's done me.

I wanted to put this story down in order, but Dick says no. Start with a bang and fill in the past through flashbacks. People will be so impressed with the first episode that they'll be willing to sit through the boring bits.

I asked Dick when he became such an expert on literature, and he shot me one of his cow-scaring looks.

So I am going to begin with the robbery of the post office in the village of Lock or I will not get any supper. I want you to imagine that it is a cold January morning. People are just starting to queue up with their pension books, and across the street in our stolen Morris Minor, Mammy is loading her Webley revolver.

Lock. South-East Ireland. 1955.

That day was my birthday. Fourteen years old. And to celebrate, Mammy was bringing me along on a job. Her first post-office robbery.

"I'm only doing this because I love you, my Winter baby," she said, slotting another bullet into the Webley revolver's chamber. "Some mothers would leave their little boys at home, but I want us to do things together.

"You are to be my blue-eyed lookout," Mammy continued, licking her fingers to smooth my hair. "If you see a fat sergeant waddling down the street, you beep the horn. Then I can be ready for him inside the door."

I didn't want to be in a criminal gang, but I didn't want to see Mammy dragged off to lady prison because I kept my smart ideas to myself either, so I said:

"One beep could be any old horn. Why don't I sound three beeps?"

Mammy leaned her forehead against mine, her blonde wig tickling my nose.

"Three beeps then, my little genius."

She tucked a few red curls under the wig, finishing the outfit with movie-star sunglasses.

I caught her hand before she could leave.

"Mammy. Don't hurt any people. Just one shot into the ceiling if any of the farmers get cocky. Promise?"

Mammy hid the pistol inside a deep pocket. "No hurting. I promise. Ceiling shots only. My present to you, my darling Charley."

I wanted to say something important.

Something clever that could change our lives.

"Mammy. This is not a movie. Being shot hurts."

At fourteen of course I knew the difference between real life and the movies, but I don't think my mother did. She propped the sunglasses on her forehead for a moment. There was a tear in one eye, hanging there like a speck of ice. This was one of my mother's favourite looks and she could summon a tear instantly. There were plenty of sad memories to draw on. "Of course this is a movie, baby. It's all a movie. We'll be happy ever after in the end. I promise."

Then she kissed her finger and rubbed it on my nose. A straight kiss on the nose would ruin her lipstick, and Mammy didn't like that. She even wore make-up to bed, in case the guards came for her.

I watched her cross the main street. Wrapped up in wartime tweed and dreams of Hollywood. Mammy once told me that she played movie soundtracks in her head when life wasn't interesting enough. I heard her hum fade as she drifted away from me.

I slid across into the driver's seat, laying my hand on the horn. Gently though. A false alarm would be a disaster. I had often played the lookout before. Outside petrol stations and chemist shops. Easy pickings, Mammy called them. The attendants never remembered anything except the movie-star smile, and maybe the revolver tickling their noses. The papers had even given Mammy a nickname: Sal Capone, they called her. Mammy liked that. She even kept the newspaper clippings in the lining of her suitcase with our stash of pound notes.

A post office.

We were sticking up a post office.

Petrol stations were one thing but some post offices had wires running straight to the police station. One fast hand on the alarm button and five minutes later they would be dragging

Mammy down the street, her high heels cutting tracks in the morning frost. It would not be like a movie. It would be like life in Ireland: cold and hard and with no happy ending. She would be thrown into a grey prison where the women's hands were raw and skinned from scrubbing, and their backs bent from hard labour.

No more powder puffs. No blood-red lipstick.

My mother was not strong enough for prison. Keeping me safe from my father had used up all her strength.

My father: a devil with knuckles like walnuts and a gold tooth that he stole from a dead man's mouth.

He was on our trail and the only way my mother could keep going was to turn our lives into a movie with a happy ending.

But there were no happy endings.

Even a fourteen-year-old boy knew that.

I pulled up my knees and sat hunkered on the driver's seat trying to concentrate on my job.

I was a lookout, I told myself, that was all.

That possibly wasn't even a sin. Being a lookout probably did not even require a visit to confession. Lookouts were more or less innocent bystanders in unusual circumstances.

I did not believe it for a second. Neither would the law. I often woke from tangle-sheet dreams where the judge I stood below in the dock would look like Mammy's favourite actor Charles Laughton, and he would bang his gavel as he laughed and laughed.

Mammy joined the tail end of a small queue trickling into the post office. The door closed behind her with the tinkle of a latch bell and the sound flitted across the street's cold still air like a winter bird.

I should not have been thinking of winter birds. I had a serious job to do.

The road: watch it for fat sergeants.

I focused on the road as though concentration beams would burst from my eyes and seek out any danger to my mother.

Danger to my mother?

She was the one with the revolver. Now that I thought about it, hadn't there been a child in that post-office line, swinging from her father's hand, hanging on to a single finger?

There were cold bullets in that gun. Mammy shot a bottle of Mercurochrome in an Offaly chemist last month. It was only a matter of time before she hit a person with real blood inside them, not crimson antiseptic.

The road. Watch it.

And I did.

Lock was not much more than a one-street town. The road was packed dirt, hardened by the cold, slick with frost. There was a village school at the far end with jostling bunches of students gathering at the gate. They were no danger to Mammy and I did not wish to think on school any more as I missed it too much. But now the memories were bobbing to the surface.

School. Mr Doran with his tin whistle and crooked smile. Calm settled over my heart like a warm blanket. Multiplication was so easy when you took it slowly. That was all you had to do. Mr Doran was funny too with all his *farmer* jokes.

I banged the steering wheel with my hand, driving away the memories of school.

I was a lookout now. School Charley was another person from another life.

Back to the road. I was Lookout Charley now.

The street was so still that it might have been a photograph. There was no wind and the Irish flag hung limply from a flagpole atop the village guesthouse. Anyone moving determinedly this way would stand out like a sore thumb, but I doubted that anyone moved with determination in this sleepy town, especially a fat sergeant with his endless cups of tea and comfortable boots.

I willed the post-office door to open and incredibly it did, but only to release two young ladies into the street. They were wrapped up against the cold, apart from their legs which flashed pale as they hurried back along the street, heads almost touching as they chatted excitedly.

Mammy had not made her move yet. And I knew why. My mother would not want young girls in the room when she pulled the Webley from her pocket. She was Sal Capone. If things went wrong Mammy would not want pretty girls getting their photographs in the paper. She was the pretty one. Mammy was the beautiful one.

Oh, Mammy. What are we going to do? Can there be a happy ending?

The door opened again and the little girl and her daddy emerged. The man was unhappy about something and stalked down the street muttering, forcing his daughter to chase behind.

Safe.

The little girl was safe at least. And the coast was still clear. I allowed myself a sigh. Maybe… Just maybe, today was not the day it all came to an end.

Someone rapped on the motor-car window and I believe I actually cried out in surprise.

"Are you the driver of the vehicle, sir?" said a voice muted by the glass and I turned my head to see a guard's tunic with a set of strong fingers interlaced in front of it.

He had come from a side lane, emerging from the shadows without a sound.

I had seen fingers like that before. Blanched by sea water and criss-crossed with scars. A fisherman's hands. The face above was just the right side of gaunt with cheekbones that would have had Mammy swooning. The eyes were sky blue and surrounded with wrinkles and lines carved there by Irish winters.

This was no fat sergeant. This was a wiry, fifty-something man of the sea who had taken up the uniform to keep the wolf from the door. Of course I was guessing about his hands. Perhaps he soaked his fingers in white vinegar to toughen them for picking guitar strings.

"Are you the driver of this vehicle?" said the guard again.

He was joking. I knew because I could see his teeth, or perhaps he planned to eat me.

I wound the window's stiff handle. "No, guard. I'm not the driver. I'm waiting for my mother."

"I won't have to arrest you then," said the guard, definitely smiling. "Just don't knock off that handbrake with your knee."

"Don't worry, Guard, I won't."

I was amazed he hadn't arrested me already. Guilt must have shown on my face.

Something showed anyway, because the policeman frowned, changing the crinkle pattern round his eyes.

He leaned his elbows on the door-frame. "Are you all right there, young fella? You look like you just took a whiff of sour milk."

I thought fast, something I had learned to do from being on the road with mother. You never knew when a quick and believable lie would keep you out of the courts.

"I have a bit of that tummy thing that's doing the rounds. That's why I'm out of school today. Mammy is running to the chemist's for some liver salts."

Mammy always says that a good lie takes care of the question that has been asked and the one to follow.

The guard's smile had a twist of sympathy in it. "Don't talk to me about that tummy yoke. I had a wrestle with that myself a few weeks ago." He winked. "Stay in a ventilated area, that's my advice."

I smiled back ruefully, like an ill boy might.

"I'll leave the window open, Guard."

The man saluted. "That's the spirit, soldier." And he was gone, trotting briskly across the road towards the post office.

Soldier? An ex-army man maybe.

Towards the post office!

I leaned on the horn, but it bleated once and died, frozen by a night spent near the river. This had happened before, why had I not remembered?

Perhaps the guard would veer off, continue on his rounds down the street.

Perhaps my blunder would not be a fatal one.

But no. Straight in he went, calling a greeting as he entered the building.

I pressed hard on the horn once more, grinding the heel of my hand into the pad but when one beep refused to sound, to expect three was idiotic.

What should I do?

Was there anything to be done?

My mother's outlaw days were over. Mine too. Where would we be sent?

Australia.

The continent's name popped into my mind, as though prisoners were still shipped down under.

No. There would be no sunny beachside detention for us. There would be the harsh granite and cold bars of Irish prisons.

I was out of the car and halfway across the street before my legs knew what orders they were following.

So I was going to the post office, was I? Graduating from lookout to full-blown accomplice. I was a minor, but the judicial system could easily decide to toss me into an adult prison, especially since I was racing to involve myself in the holding up of a government building.

But it was my mother and we loved each

other so what choice did I have?

I lurched across the road, limbs tense, anticipating a gunshot. But there was no crack but the cracking of morning ice under my feet, announcing my arrival.

What could I do? Where were my brilliant ideas now? Three beeps on a frozen horn. This was my fault.

A shameful voice rose in my head. Craven and selfish.

Run. Take the pound notes from the suitcase and board the ferry to England.

But I was not low enough for that path, or perhaps I was too much of a coward. So I shouldered the post-office door and stumbled inside.

It was bad.

But there was no blood so far as I could see. Customers were lined up along the walls, their eyes glued to the strange sight of a rural guard pinning a city girl to a wall, both of her small hands easily contained by one of his fisherman's mitts. The guard seemed relaxed as though he had done this kind of thing many times before but the easy smile of minutes ago had been wiped away by the whole business.

My mother's wig was askew and her lipstick smeared along the wall, like an extension of her mouth. She had her brave face on.

"What are you up to?" the guard was asking my mother, as though he had caught his daughter filching a shilling. "Are times so hard?"

One of the customers, a young man wearing boots too big for his feet, clapped his hands once, trapping a memory.

"That's her. From the newspaper. Sal Capone." He fluttered his fingers at the post mistress. "You have a picture of her on the board, Brigit."

It was true. There she was. My mother. Pinned to a notice board between a second-hand bicycle and a missing greyhound.

Mammy was horrified. "That is not a good picture. Look at me, for heaven's sake."

But they looked at the notice board. All except me. I was gazing at the counter-top upon which sat a Webley revolver, put out of mother's reach by the guard. It had spun on the surface, the cylinder scratching circles in the wood like a skate on ice.

Out of mother's reach but not out of mine.

No one was looking.

I grabbed the gun and its weight was not a shock to me. Mother had made me practise many times in foggy dawn forests.

"Let her go," I said, not loudly enough because not a single person turned.

So I forced some volume into it the next time.

"I said let her go!"

The guard's eyes swept across the counter-top and onwards to me, and he put the whole thing together in a second. I suppose it didn't take a genius.

"Feeling better, are you, boy?"

"No," I said miserably. And it was true. I felt considerably worse.

The guard held my mother in place expertly, almost casually. I suppose she was about as much trouble as a sparrow compared to the rowdy weekend deep-sea fishermen he no doubt regularly subdued.

"Let her go, or you shoot? That's the long and short of it, I suppose?"

I nodded. No more speaking unless necessary. I'd have to work on my *giving orders* voice if the chance arose.

The guard nodded at my pistol. "The thing about guns is that if you're not used to them..."

I did not need to speak to deal with this. I cocked the revolver, sighted along the barrel and flicked off the safety with my thumb.

The post office's customers screamed in unison, a choir of terror, and I could feel them getting ready to charge the door. They would trample me, someone could get hurt.

"Nobody move a muscle," said the guard and I had to admit to myself at least that his voice of authority was a lot better than mine.

"Now, son," he said to me. "Put down the gun. You're nabbed. It's for the best."

My mother craned her face round. "Don't listen to him, Charley. This is not the right time. Dublin, that's where they will catch us. Or even London."

The guard whistled and I knew what he meant.

Dublin?

London?

Mother was planning for us to go down in a hail of gunfire.

"Mammy, this can't go on for ever."

My mother's eyes were bright. "Of course it can. Of course. They will remember us for ever. Mother and son, it's never been done before."

I realised then that my mother as I knew her, the one who hid me behind her skirts, the one who taught me the names of flowers, was gone. She was lost to me.

Somehow the guard knew what to say.

"There's no happy ending here, son, just the best of a bad lot."

He was right. I was never going to shoot anyone.

"Don't listen to him," my mother screeched. I had never heard her screech before. "Not here. There isn't a single camera."

The guard's face was grim. "I have a lovely camera down in the station."

This quip almost changed my mind and my hands stiffened with resolve.

"That's enough chitchat, Charles!" called Mother. "Shoot him. Just in the leg. We need to get on the road before this building is surrounded. Don't you see that?"

"You are nothing but a lookout," said the

guard, holding my eye. "A minor waiting in the car like his mammy told him. I guarantee you will not be prosecuted and your mother hasn't hurt anyone yet. But if you shoot me, or anyone, in any part of the body, then you both go to prison for a long time. As it is, you'll be fostered for a while and could be reunited with your mother in a couple of years."

"Really?" This sounded optimistic.

"Maybe five," admitted the guard.

The entire post office held its breath. What would the lookout boy do?

I think Mother had enough sense left to know she was losing me.

"Shoot me then, Charley. I don't mind. Then another family could look after you. If you shoot me, it's even better than the police doing it. I'll be international news."

This movie was over. They should never have started rolling without a happy ending.

I put the gun down on the counter-top and

a building sighed with relief.

"No, Charles," my mother screeched again. "No. There is nothing glamorous about this. Nothing."

She was right. Her make-up was ruined, the light was terrible and Mammy's shapely legs were masked by the guard.

He picked up the gun without releasing my mother.

"Walk ahead of me," he said not unkindly. "Up to the station."

I was numb, apart from my heart, which felt as though it was connected to an air pump. My mother had set her face to heroic disappointment, which was one of her favourites and I knew she would not even acknowledge me for at least a few days.

The guard ushered us both out the door and something in my expression must have reminded him of the tragic story of his own family that I was to find out about much later.

"Don't worry, boy. There's surely some fool who will take you in. No workhouse for you, my word on it."

His promise didn't mean much then but it would come to be a turning point in my life.

A customer patted the guard's shoulder as we passed.

"Good job, Dick. You handled that like a pro."

"I am a pro," said Dick the guard with one of his cow-scaring looks, and the door opened before us, admitting a cold gust of winter's breath.

The Snow Globe

Marita Conlon-McKenna

Illustrated by

P.J. Lynch

Marita Conlon-McKenna is one of Ireland's best-loved authors. Her award-winning novels for children include *Under the Hawthorn Tree*, which has been translated into over a dozen languages, and *The Blue Horse*, both number one bestsellers. *Under the Hawthorne Tree* was also televised for Irish, British and American audiences. Marita lives in Dublin.

P. J. Lynch has been working as an illustrator for over twenty-five years and has won many awards in that time, including the Mother Goose Award and the prestigious Kate Greenaway Medal on two occasions. P. J. lives in Dublin with his wife and their three children.

I hate the new house.

I hate the way it looks, I hate the way it smells and most of all I hate that it is miles and miles away from where I used to live and all my friends.

"It's a nice city, Cass. You'll get used to it and the new school is only a few minutes away from our house. Honestly, you'll like it."

Honestly I won't, because I never wanted to move and leave Rosemount Park, the place where we used to live! But Dad's plant in Kildare closed down and he was one of the lucky ones that got transferred to the company's new plant in Galway.

"Why couldn't Dad just go and come back home to us at the weekends?"

"Because we are a family and families stick together," Mum said crossly.

So now we are living in Galway in an old house that is practically falling down. The windows rattle and my bedroom is up on the third floor. From it I can see the street and part of the river. Our garden is long and narrow and overgrown.

"Next summer we'll tackle it," Dad promises.

The house is full of paint tins and ladders and boxes and Mum says we have to put in a new kitchen as the old one has woodworm.

It's only a few days to Christmas and I wish I was back with Sophie and Alanna, hanging out on our estate and seeing all my friends instead of being stuck here being dragged round the garden centre with Mum and Dad trying to get a Christmas tree. The ceiling in our living room is really high so we buy a tree that is much taller than usual and we can hardly fit it in our car. It makes the house smell of fresh pine.

Dad and Robbie search all the boxes, wondering where the movers have put our Christmas decorations. They find one box with some lights and our stockings and a few baubles but the rest have gone missing. We hang what we have on the tree and Ted puts the angel on top but it looks bare… like the house.

"We'll buy some more," says Mum as we switch on the lights. "Doesn't it look wonderful? It's as if these old bay windows were meant for Christmas trees."

I say nothing.

"Cass, don't you think it's so exciting having a first Christmas in our new house?"

"I'd much prefer Christmas in our old house with our friends and the neighbours," I say.

Mum looks upset.

"Cass, that's quite enough!" Dad warns. "Listen, why don't you and Robbie walk over to the square? There's a big open-air Christmas market there. Buy a few presents, and for heaven's sake try to get in the Christmas spirit?" He passes us each some money.

"Thanks, Dad." My older brother grins, putting the cash in his pocket.

"Thanks," I say.

On the way to the square we pass gangs of shoppers carrying bags and two groups of carol singers. The streets are busy and it is really cold… so cold it might even snow.

Eyre Square is all lit up and it really is Christmassy with wooden stalls and even a big log cabin. There is a café with red-and-white tablecloths and lots of chairs and some braziers burning. We buy long German hot dogs and have them with mustard and cabbage and they taste so good. One stall is selling giant pretzels and another has yummy hot doughnuts.

"We'll get one later," Robbie promises as we walk on. "I want to get Dad a present."

He stops at a stall that has a collection of knitted hats and scarves. Rob pulls on a camouflage army one, and I try a cute pink stripy one. We wonder if Dad would like the dark green one. He could wear it when he goes to matches – Dad's mad on football and rugby.

We decide it'd be perfect, so Robbie pays for it and then goes off in search of more presents.

"We should split up," he says, and I guess that he wants to find something for me.

I head off in another direction. It has begun to snow lightly, the flakes floating in the air like feathers and tumbling gently to the ground before melting.

There are stalls full of toys and games and people selling jams and sauces and home-made cakes and biscuits. I walk towards the back. One lady is selling printed scarves. They look pretty… I wonder if Mum would like one.

Then I see it. There is an old woman with a stall full of bric-a-brac. Old Dinky cars still in their boxes, stiff porcelain dolls with white painted faces. They look kind of scary but a lady picks up one and pays for it. I watch as the old woman wraps it in tissue carefully.

"Her name is Violet," she says. "And she is a very special doll… remember that."

The old woman has white hair scrunched up with a silver comb and eyes so dark they are like two black beetles. I look at the brooches and bracelets, and an old snakes-and-ladders game, and then I see it, right at the back of the stall… a snow globe. I pick it up. It is heavier than I expected. The glass is thick and the dark wood base is patterned with silver holly leaves and berries.

Inside the glass orb there is a girl with dark hair and a red dress and beside her a tree and a deer. I shake the globe and like magic the snow appears and the tree sparkles and the girl's dress seems to glow and the deer is covered with falling snowflakes. It's beautiful.

I shake it again. As the snow falls I notice a small rabbit peeping out from behind the tree and a robin in its branches. It's so pretty. I look at the price… Far too much.

"It's Victorian," the old woman says, standing in front of me. "Antique."

"It's beautiful."

A man pushes in beside me. He wants to buy the red velvet box with four dice in it.

"These dice will bring you luck!" says the old woman as he passes her the money.

I shake the snow globe again. It's so unusual, special. I watch as the snow slowly begins to

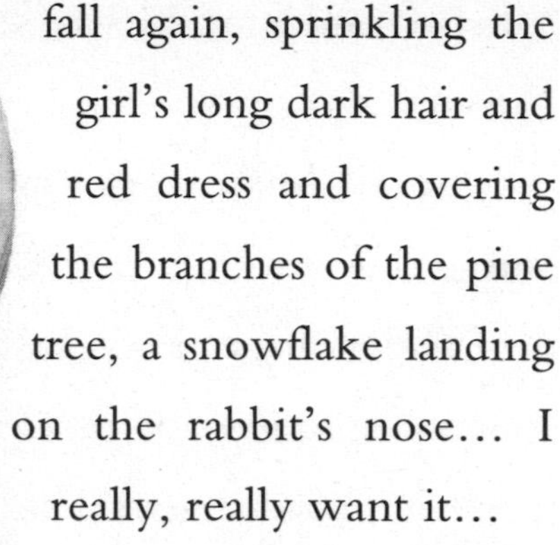

fall again, sprinkling the girl's long dark hair and red dress and covering the branches of the pine tree, a snowflake landing on the rabbit's nose... I really, really want it...

"How much money do you have?" the woman asks, standing so close to me that I can smell her old-fashioned lavender-scented perfume.

Before I know it I have agreed to buy the precious snow globe and given her all my money and she is wrapping it up in lots of paper and passing me a plastic bag.

"It's really old," she warns me, "so you must take very good care of it. It's full of wishing and memories."

I walk off happy...

"Where have you been?" demands Robbie

when I find him. "I was searching everywhere for you."

"Sorry, but I was at that old antique stall at the back."

"Did you get all your presents?" he asks as we queue to get doughnuts.

I've already got Robbie a game for his PlayStation. They were on special offer in Argos last week. And I've got Dad a tie covered in balls – footballs, golf balls, rugby balls – that I saw in the sports store, but I've got nothing for Mum or our little brother Ted.

"I forgot," I admit to Robbie.

"Well come on and we'll get something now."

"I can't," I confess. "I've spent all my money."

I show him the snow globe.

"Is it for Mum?"

"No, Mum wouldn't like it! It's for me – I just had to have it!"

"Cass, are you crazy? How could you spend all your money on that?"

I suddenly realise how stupid I've been. Money is tight with the move and the new house, so this year there is a family budget on presents and I've blown all my money on one thing.

"Maybe you can take it back – get your money back."

Robbie and I return to the edge of the square, looking for the old woman and her stall. We pass the people selling jam and big iced gingerbread houses, but I can't seem to find the place where I got the snow globe. I walk up and down, looking for the old-fashioned wooden stall with its fairy lights and mysterious owner.

"Where is it?" asks Robbie.

"It was here, I'm sure it was here..."

But there is no sign of it – just a stand with a man selling burgers and drinks.

"It was here, I'm sure," I say.

"What are you going to do?" he asks, sighing.

I don't know what to do. I can't ask Dad for more money, not at the moment.

"I've some money left – I can lend it to you," Robbie offers. "But you'll have to give it back to me. Promise?"

I promise.

The square is getting darker as we walk back to the stand with the patterned scarves, and Robbie helps me pick out one for Mum. I also get her a silver ball for the tree with 'Best mum' written on it.

Then we see a man and a woman selling hand and string puppets and I've just enough money left to buy an amazing dragon one for Ted. He loves dragons and always wants me to make up stories about them.

"That everything?" asks Robbie as we set off back home.

The snow has eased up but my face and hands are still freezing.

When we're outside the house I can see the lights from our Christmas tree and the glow of coloured glass at the top of our front door.

Back inside, I run upstairs to my room, hide my presents and go down to help.

Mum is baking in the kitchen. She's making mince pies and biscuits and Ted has an apron on and is all covered with flour.

Soon there are trays of mince pies and star-shaped biscuits in the oven and the house is filled with their smell.

"I hope they don't burn," worries Mum. "Old ovens can be temperamental. I can't wait to get my new kitchen in a few months' time."

We have lasagne and chips for dinner. Ted's worried that Santa won't know that he has moved house. We all promise him that will not happen.

"Remember we sent him a letter?" says Mum as Ted gets dressed into his pyjamas.

I phone Alanna. She and Sophie are going carol singing with a load of girls from my old class in the shopping centre to raise money for an orphanage in Africa.

"You'll make friends, Cass, honestly you will," says Alanna, but I know I'll never have friends like them again. I feel so lonely.

I unwrap my snow globe and put it carefully on the dressing table. It is so beautiful and I give it a slow, gentle shake and watch the snow fall and tumble and swirl gently around inside. It's like magic, with the girl and the snow and the deer and the rabbit… I love it.

I watch TV for a while, then I go to bed. I can't sleep. I keep thinking about our old house. We always had a big lit-up Santa in our front garden and on Christmas Eve went next door to Tommy and Linda's. On Christmas Day all our relations would call and then come over for dinner, the kids at one table and the grown-ups at another... But this Christmas it's going to be awful!

My room is freezing cold. There is a draught from the window and I get up to make sure it is fully closed. It is, but the windows are so old and they rattle. Dad says we'll have new ones when we can afford them. I pull on a fleece hoodie over my pyjamas. I shake my snow globe and as the snow begins to fall and fall I wish that this Christmas could be like last year's... The robin is there on the branch of the tree, the girl is holding her hands up to the snow.

I fall asleep for a while and when I wake it's very dark and the room even colder. I dare not breathe as I feel cold snowflakes swirl around my bed. The moonlight falls on the snow globe and I can see the girl with the long dark hair in her red dress catch the snowflakes. She looks at me. Her skin is white, as white as snow, and her eyes are dark as coal and it seems like my room is filled with snow.

"Come," she whispers.

I walk downstairs and can see the living room is bright and the massive Christmas tree in the window is covered in baubles and lights. The fire is blazing and swags of holly and ivy hang from the mantelpiece where candles glow.

I cannot believe it – the room looks so different. There are bright patterned cushions and a massive footstool and a big plush plum-coloured velvet couch where our old brown one usually goes.

Then I see her, the girl with the long dark hair like my own, laughing and hanging some glass ornaments from the Christmas-tree branches. They seem to shine and catch the light. A star, a moon, a deer, a rabbit, a small glass robin, each tied with a piece of red ribbon. The door to the dining room is open and I can see the big table set with plates and cutlery and glasses. Two huge candelabras highlight the table filled with food and I watch as the girl runs in to sit down…

Suddenly, the door closes and I'm back upstairs. The house is quiet except for Dad, who I can hear snoring, loudly and rhythmically, like he always does.

"For heaven's sake, get up, Cass!" orders Mum. "Granny and Granddad have just phoned to say that Sandra's boys are sick with chickenpox, so I've invited them to come and stay with us for Christmas instead… They'll be here tomorrow."

I can't believe it, my wish is coming true! Granny and Granddad are coming here on Christmas Day and we'll be together! I run downstairs and grab some juice and some toast and Mum gives us a list of things to do.

"I want the house to look good," Mum frowns, "and feel warm and cosy and welcoming."

That's going to be hard, as the heating isn't

working properly and half our stuff is still in boxes.

"Cass, can you check some of the boxes upstairs? We need to find the good dinner plates and cutlery, and the white duvet-cover set for Granny and Granddad's bed. I'll put them in Robbie's room and he can sleep in the bunk room with Ted."

I know that the movers put some boxes in the small storage room near where I sleep, so I go to check there.

One half of the room is taken up with the cardboard boxes. I open one or two but they are mostly filled with clothes and shoes and summer stuff – beach towels and swimsuits and the parasol – though there's also a box of books.

From the storage room there are steps leading up to the attic – maybe I'll find what I'm looking for there. The light isn't working and it's gloomy and almost black as I walk up the stairs.

I leave the door open wide. The attic smells musty. There is an old lamp and a crate or two, a rolled-up carpet and some old furniture. I watch a big spider scuttle along the floorboards. I am about to go back downstairs when I see her… the girl in the red dress. She is very faint, shimmering, and snowflakes fall around her as she sits on an old wooden chest watching me. I should be scared but I'm not. She smiles at me and I feel like we are friends. It's as if she wants me to look around the attic.

As I turn around I almost fall over a big brown box. It has 'Dinner Set' written in black marker on it.

"I've found the plates and cutlery!" I yell and Mum comes upstairs to join me in the attic.

"It's cold up here but at least it's good and dry," she says, looking round in the gloom at what is stored and hidden up here. Suddenly she spots the old couch and footstool.

"Look at these, Cass!" she says, excited. "They must have been left behind when the house was sold.

"They used to be in the drawing room," I blurt out, recognising the plum-coloured couch.

"Imagine that," says Mum, smiling. "Hidden away up here, they're worn and threadbare but otherwise perfect. When we get some money we'll get them reupholstered and covered and use them back in the drawing room."

Mum and I carry the heavy box downstairs and unpack it and wash all our good plates and bowls for Christmas dinner tomorrow. Robbie and Ted and I spend the rest of the day helping Mum and Dad. I wrap my presents and put them under the tree. We stay up late watching Christmas movies and Dad makes popcorn.

There is a full moon when I am going to bed, which makes the street and the river outside my window look like silver. Without thinking, I pick up my snow globe and ever so slowly turn it upside down, watching the snow gently fall, covering the tree and the deer and the girl… There is something so weird and strange and special about it. I give it a really good shake and the snow falls faster as the tree is iced with white and the girl's fingers try to grasp it and the deer has snowflakes on his nose.

I look at the girl. *She's just a girl in a glass bubble*, I tell myself over and over again. I wish that I could stop missing my friends and our old house so much.

The snow falls… and the room gets colder and colder.

When I open my eyes the girl in the red dress is standing near my window looking at the moon, the robin perched beside her.

"Don't be scared," she says. "I'm your friend."

I watch as the room fills with snow.

"You will not be lonely here in this house!" she says and laughs, her breath cold as ice.

When I wake she is gone.

★

On Christmas morning there is a new bike for me, a phone for Robbie, and Ted gets a huge Lego castle with a dungeon and dragons and soldiers. Then, after a big breakfast, we all walk to church.

"What a beautiful old house," says Granny, when she and Granddad arrive later on, laden down with presents and wine and a big plum pudding. "It must be full of history and memories."

Granddad admires the bay windows and the stairs and the fireplace, and Granny loves their bedroom with its tall windows and high ceilings, and the old-fashioned bathroom with the long flush toilet chain.

We all gather round the tree to open our presents. The fairy lights sparkle, the fire is blazing and the house is warm at last as the plumber came late last night and fixed the heating. Robbie and

I cut down branches of holly and ivy from our garden to decorate the hall and stairs and the mantelpiece and dining room.

Robbie gives me the cute pink hat from the market, and a set of biscuit cutters. Dad puts on his new tie and Mum loves the scarf I gave her and Ted calls his dragon puppet Max! Granny and Granddad have got presents for us too, with a really big one for Mum and Dad. It's a pair of silver candelabras.

"They've been in the family for years," confesses Granddad, "but we thought with an old house like this they would be perfect."

"Thank you," says Mum, "they are beautiful. I'll put them on the table."

Ted's given a remote-control car and Robbie a really cool pair of earphones that he has wanted for ages.

Then Granny passes me a box.

Curious, I open it. Inside there are six perfect glass Christmas ornaments. I lift them out carefully – two robins, a rabbit and a deer, and a star and moon, each threaded with a loop of red ribbon. I can't believe it!

"Granny, they are beautiful! Where did you get them?"

"I saw them in a shop window and thought they were so pretty I couldn't resist them."

It's like some kind of strange magic is happening as Ted helps me to hang each one on our tree.

Mum is busy getting the dinner ready and Robbie and I set the oak dining table with our Christmas tablecloth and the china serving dishes and Dad puts the tall white candles in the candelabras in the centre. The room looks just the way I saw it before…

Sitting down to Christmas dinner the candles flicker and are reflected in our big mirror as we eat plates of turkey and ham and stuffing followed by mince pies and some of

Granny's pudding.

Afterwards we play charades and watch TV as Granddad dozes in the armchair. I can't believe that we have had our first Christmas in the new house… I almost phone Alanna and Sophie but decide to wait until tomorrow.

"It's snowing!" Dad calls and we all run to the window to watch.

It's coming down really heavily, covering the path and the street outside.

"The weather forecast says it could last for days," he tells us, and it does, lasting all week.

Everything looks so different, icy and white – our house and the garden and the street and the town. We make snowmen and have snowball fights with some of the neighbours. Granny and Granddad stay until after the New Year, our house crowded and noisy, beginning to feel like home.

Now I am getting ready for bed, the night before

I go to my new school. I'm really nervous about it.

I shake the snow globe hard so the snow is almost like a snowstorm, watching it swirl and move so I can barely see the girl in the red dress and the deer and the rabbit.

"I wish that school will be OK."

I wake in the middle of the night feeling cold. It's like I am in a blizzard and I can see inside a big building with corridors and classrooms. I see desks and a whiteboard and rows and rows of students. I feel scared. Then I hear voices floating up in the air, singing…

I hold my breath. She is there again – the snow at her feet, the deer standing nervously beside her. I knew she would come…

"Don't be afraid," she whispers slowly. "I am always here…"

In the morning I get dressed and put on my new school uniform. I wish that I didn't have to go to school but Ted is starting too. Mum is taking him as she wants to settle him in with his new teacher and class.

I am standing at the front door waiting for them when I see a girl coming out of the house a few doors away from us. She is wearing the same navy-and-grey uniform as me. She smiles at me and walks over.

"You starting at St Paul's?" she asks.

I nod.

"I'm in class six; which class are you in?"

"Six."

"You just move into the house? I knew the old lady who lived there – she died last year."

"We moved in a few days before Christmas. My dad's got a new job here."

"We went to my nan's in Scotland for Christmas but with the bad weather we only got home three days ago," she explains. "By the way, my name is Ella."

"And I'm Cass."

"Are you ready to go now?"

"I have to wait for my little brother."

"Well I'd better go but I'll see you later." She smiles. Ella's got braces and has short curly hair and I immediately like her.

Ted is taking ages and Mum has his lunch box in her hand as she locks the front door.

"You OK?" I ask him. He must be scared too.

"I couldn't find him," sighs Mum. "Do you know where he was? Upstairs in your bedroom playing with your snow globe thing."

"I just wanted to shake the snow," he protests. "I didn't break it, Cass – I just wanted to see the rabbit again."

"The little rabbit in the snow is cute!" I agree.

"I just needed to see him again before school so he'd make everything be all right."

"See the rabbit?"

He's walking beside me with his Transformers schoolbag.

"When you shake the glass it's magic," he whispers, so Mum can't hear. "I see him sometimes when my room is snowy. The rabbit hides under my bed so I won't be scared in the new house. He showed me our garden with a big swing and said he'll be there when I get home to tell him all about school."

I can feel my heart beat fast… thinking of the snow globe, thinking of the swirling snowflakes and the girl in the red dress… waiting for me…

The King of the Birds

MICHAEL SCOTT

Illustrated by
Chris Haughton

Michael Scott writes for both adults and young adults. He is considered one of the authorities on Celtic folklore and his collections, *Irish Folk & Fairy Tales*, *Irish Myths & Legends* and *Irish Ghosts & Hauntings*, have been in print for the past twenty years. His *New York Times* bestselling YA series, The Secrets of the Immortal Nicholas Flamel, is available in over twenty languages and thirty-eight countries.

Chris Haughton is an Irish designer and illustrator. His first book, *A Bit Lost*, is available in nineteen languages and has won many awards including the Dutch Picture Book of the Year. Chris's latest and third Picture Book is *Shh! We Have a Plan* and was published in 2014. Chris's aim is to create children's books that can be read without words, so that children from across the world can understand everything just by looking at them. Chris lives in London.

In Ireland, December 26th is called Wren Day (La an Dreoilín), and the tiny bird has always occupied a special place in Irish mythology. Although the wren is the smallest of birds, it is sometimes called the King of the Birds.

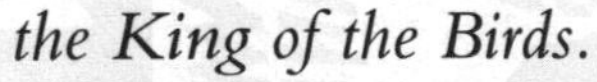

There is a song that begins, "The wren, the wren, the king of all birds…"

But how did such a tiny

creature become the ruler of all the birds of the air?

In the still pre-dawn air, the bare frost-speckled winter trees were lined with birds.

Every glittering branch bowed beneath the weight of flocks that had gathered from all across Ireland, and the trees were alive with the whispering rasp of their feathers. The birds had kept to their own kin: the blackbirds and cuckoos clustered together, while the smaller birds – the sparrows, robins and thrushes, starlings and swallows – swarmed the upper branches. The lower branches groaned beneath the weight of some of the bigger birds – the falcons and ospreys – while gulls, cormorants and the other seabirds moved across the hard-frozen earth, feet rasping on the thin covering of ice.

It was the winter solstice, the shortest day of the year, and the birds of Ireland had assembled to choose their ruler.

Boar, oxen, cats and dogs and even the deer had their rulers, but no one had claimed kingship over the birds, and for generations they had been ruled by a squabbling Parliament, mostly composed of black-eyed crows and nervous irritable robins. They could never agree on anything. Finally, the Parliament had turned to Relige, the ancient barn owl, for advice. No one knew how old he was. It was rumoured he had actually seen the birth of the world when it was pushed up from the ocean floor and that he had carried the first seeds to plant the great forests of oak, ash and yew that now blanketed the land. Even the fearsome two-legged humani acknowledged the owl's wisdom.

Relige had spent months flying from flock to flock, listening as each one claimed the right to rule. He knew if he simply picked a ruler it would solve nothing: the other bird flocks would not acknowledge them as their leader. Finally, he decided that the only way to choose a king would be by a trial of flight that would be open to all.

Thousands of sparrow messengers had flitted across the country carrying the news: the king would be chosen on the day of the winter solstice. Any birds interested in challenging for the leadership were to gather at Eo Mugna, the Great Oak at the mouth of the River Shannon and one of the Five Sacred Trees of Ireland.

"Only a few will contest the kingship," Eala, one of the two snow-white swans, said to Relige. "A lot of the smaller birds will not even bother trying."

The swans, like the owl, had no interest in the kingship, and would act as judges.

"No, there will be more," Aela, her mate, said.

"Everyone believes they can be the king."

"All the birds of Ireland will come," Relige said with a solemn nod. "If not to take part, then *tooo* observe and simply *tooo* be able to say that they were there when the king was chosen. Thousands will come," he hooted.

The day of the solstice dawned bitterly cold, the air from the ice lands at the top of the world carrying flecks of ice and the promise of snow. The birds started to gather just before the dawn. They arrived singly and in pairs, in long trailing V's across the grey sky or in huge wheeling flocks that moved as one.

Relige sat in the heart of the ancient Eo Mugna with all the flocks around, above and below him. He opened his huge eyes and blinked at the gathered birds. He had been right:

there were thousands – *no*, there were tens of thousands gathered in the vast and ancient tree. The owl would referee the race and make sure that everyone observed the rule: to fly high and outlast all the others. But Relige, Eala and Aela were looking for more than strength and endurance. The king of the birds would have to be cunning and wise and, more importantly, would have to be respected by all the others.

Relige flapped his wings a few times, and gradually the muttering, chattering and twittering died down. Thousands of pairs of eyes – small, hard and black or big, bright and luminous – turned to look at him.

"Now, *youuu* all know the rules," he hooted. "Wh*oo*ever outlasts all others and flies the highest will be crowned the king of the birds. We are looking for courage and heart. We want a king who is both clever and strong. We are looking for a leader."

A feathery rustle of excitement rang through the trees.

"Aela, Eala and I will crown the king when the race has run its course," Relige continued. "Anyone found cheating will immediately be disqualified," he added sternly. Although his body remained still, his huge head spun to look over at the magpies and rooks. They shuffled back and forth on a branch, suddenly deciding to preen their blue-black feathers as they tried, and failed, to look innocent. The two huge swans on the ground beneath Relige turned to glare threateningly at them. The spectacularly plumaged black-and-white birds were extremely unreliable and notorious thieves.

"Now, are *youuu* all ready?"

Wings opened and closed and for a moment it looked as if the Great Oak and the surrounding trees had come alive with splashes of colour as a multitude of feathers shone and glistened in the grey morning light.

"Any last questions?" Relige asked, head swivelling left to right and back again.

There was a sudden cracking snap above and a twig, heavy with acorns, dropped through the higher branches of the ancient oak to the ground below. The assembled birds gasped: it was forbidden to break any leaves or branches from the sacred tree. Silence fell over the forest. Then, bronze feathers appeared through the leaves above and a sharp-beaked head thrust forward. Bright golden eyes looked down on the assembled birds, before finally turning to fix on Relige.

"I have a question."

"The assembly recognises Iolar," Eala honked loudly.

"What is your question?" Relige asked.

Iolar the Golden Eagle ruffled his magnificent feathers and spread his wings to their fullest extent. "Why are we even having this contest? Everyone knows I am the king of the birds.

Why not just crown me now?" he demanded. For such a big bird, he had a high and shrill voice, and it made him sound rather petulant.

"We will crown you if you win," Relige said patiently. He knew that the Golden Eagle already considered himself the king of the birds, and that he had bullied some of the smaller flocks into acknowledging him as their ruler.

Snag, the one-eyed Lord of the Magpies, hopped to the end of a branch and glared upwards, his single black eye fixing on the huge eagle. "How do you know you'll win?" he demanded.

A murmur of agreement ran through the flocks.

Iolar's laugh was a discordant squawk. He spread his wings wide again and they stretched almost the length of the branch he was perched on. "I am a Golden Eagle," he said. "I am the largest, the most powerful and the most beautiful bird here. I deserve to win." He closed his wings with a cracking snap and the wind buffeted a few of the smaller birds from the branches above his head, sending them spinning to the ground.

"Being big, powerful and beautiful does not give you the right to win." The owl raised one smoothly feathered wing. "Remember, Iolar, a king must be kind and considerate: speed, power and beauty alone do not make a ruler."

"But I will still win," Iolar insisted defiantly. His big head turned, eyes darting at the smaller birds as if defying them to race against him. "There are none here who can compete with me. And none who *should* compete against me," he added threateningly.

"You are a bully," a tiny voice chirruped from the shadows.

"A challenger?" Iolar glared into the thicket of leaves. "Show yourself, if you dare."

A leaf twisted and a tiny brown wren appeared.

Iolar's beak opened and closed in astonishment,

but no sounds came out.

"I am Dreolin the Wren, and I challenge you."

A few of the smaller birds cackled in amusement, but the rest remained silent. The tiny and mysterious wrens swarmed unnoticed across many lands, absorbing customs, myth and lore. They got into places off limits to larger birds and animals and were reputed to know the language of the humani.

"Enough!" Relige hooted long and loud, the sound echoing like a horn in the dawn air. "Now, *youuu* must all remember," the barn owl said, "this is not a race. Yes, flying high is important, but we are also looking for strength, skill, endurance and strategy. *Soo*, take *youuu*r time." He paused and raised his wings again.

"Are you almost ready…?"

The flocks shuffled and settled on the branches.

"Are you nearly ready…?"

They fell silent and the forest grew hushed.

"Are you ready…?"

A sparrow suddenly darted up in a flurry of wings, realised its mistake and fell back with an embarrassed cheep.

"Fly!"

With the sound of thunder, the huge flock of birds took off in an enormous cloud, rising up into the chill solstice morning sky. Branches shook and rattled as if in a storm and leaves twisted loose and swirled away. Some of the smaller trees around the ancient oak were stripped bare.

Relige and the swans, Eala and Aela, stared up at the flock of birds winging its way upwards.

"The Golden Eagle will win," Eala said. "He will be insufferable."

"He hasn't won yet," Relige said. Settling on to the branch, he wrapped his wings tightly round his body and closed his eyes.

"I will be king." Iolar's huge wings beat smoothly

and strongly, pulling him upwards. He chanted in time with the beating of his wings. "I will be king. I will be king."

Initially, the smaller lighter birds had risen first, little wings flapping furiously, but they were soon overtaken by the bigger birds, their larger wings carrying them up with slow powerful strokes. The small birds were careful not to fly beneath them – the downdraught from their wings could send them spinning out of the air.

"I will be king. I will be king."

Already, Iolar had left most of the smaller birds behind and, as he looked down, he could see that some of them were beginning to spiral back to the earth. They were exhausted with the effort and they knew it was useless to go any further.

The eagle's wings snapped wide, catching the wind, feeling it smooth and liquid beneath his feathers. Opening his beak, he called in triumph as he soared upwards. "I will be king."

He was going to win. He was going to be the

king of all the birds in Ireland.

Iolar continued climbing. Beneath him the ground curved away smoothly at the edges, the green and silver of the frost-covered land turning into the sharp blue of the sea. The eagle could make out the tiny patchwork squares of fields and the thin white threads of the roads cutting across the landscape. In the distance, on the coast, he could see a dirty smudge that was a collection of wood and mud huts – a humani village. Soon, even they would have to acknowledge him as king.

"I will be king."

Iolar flew through clouds. The white fluffy balls looked so warm and soft, but were always damp and cold. A dusting of water droplets dappled his wings like jewels.

He rose higher still.

Soon, there was no one beneath him. A seagull had hung on for a surprisingly long time, but had given up as the sun began to rise on this, the shortest day of the year. The seagull had slowly drifted back to the ground leaving Iolar alone in the sky: he was the king of the birds.

"I am the king," he said. "I am the king of the birds."

On the ground Relige and the two swans watched the distant black dot rising high, high, higher into the sky. All around Eo Mugna, the Great Oak, birds were resting, lining the branches and bushes, gathered in small groups on the hard ground. They too were looking up, watching the eagle soar into the heavens. And, as the last solitary black-headed seagull fell back to earth, leaving the Golden Eagle alone in the skies, it was clear that Iolar would be king.

There was no point in going any further. He had won. Tilting to one side, Iolar began to fall back towards the earth. When he was closer to the earth, he would close his wings and plummet shockingly fast, frightening the smaller birds. At the very last minute he would open his great wings and stop, hang in the air and then drop lightly on to a branch. It would be a dramatic demonstration of his power.

The eagle twitched.

Something moved in the feathers on his back. He shrugged. It would blow off as he fell through the icy air.

He felt it move again. And then a familiar tiny voice said cheekily, "Thank you."

Iolar twisted his head in time to see Dreolin the wren take flight off his back, wings beating furiously as it rose up into the sky. It began to sing, a delicate triumphant sound.

Iolar shouted and opened his wings, beating them furiously to catch the wind. But he was exhausted and had already dropped quite far, while the wren, who had hitched the ride on his back, was far, far above him, and rising fast on fresh wings.

"Come back," Iolar shouted. "Come back.

That's not fair. I've won."

Dreolin peered down, eyes twinkling mischievously. "Not yet you haven't. Catch me if you can."

The wren continued rising higher and higher. The eagle desperately attempted to catch up, but its wings were tired, each flap becoming more of an effort. He began to drop lower, slipping further away from the still-rising wren.

"Just you wait," he whined.

The wren flew higher, singing, singing, singing.

Furious, Iolar plummeted towards the ground, only opening his wings a few feet above the soil. They snapped him to a stop and he slid to a halt before the barn owl, long talons digging grooves into the frost-speckled earth.

"Not fair. Not fair," he attempted to shout, but it came out as a shrill shriek. "That's not fair. He cheated."

Relige smiled and looked from the furious eagle up to the tiny bird flying far above their heads. The wren dipped and spun in an intricate dance, snatches of its song carried down on the wind.

The barn owl looked at the two swans on either side of them and they whispered together for a few moments.

"Well?" Iolar demanded.

"Being a king means not only being big and strong and powerful, it also means being clever and thinking ahead and planning," Relige said. "The wren did that." The barn owl drew in a deep breath, puffing out his chest. "From this day forth," Relige announced loudly, voice echoing and re-echoing through the ancient forests, "Dreolin the wren is the king of the birds of Ireland."

And abruptly the ancient forest came alive to the vast flock singing, "*The wren, the wren, the king of all birds…*"

The Battle of the Ice Queen

GORDON SNELL

Illustrated by
Michael Emberley

Gordon Snell is a writer and broadcaster, and the author of more than forty books for children and adults, published in Ireland, England, Australia, Canada and the United States. He also writes song lyrics, musicals and opera librettos for the stage, and for BBC and RTE radio and television. He lives in Dalkey, County Dublin.

Michael Emberley was born near Boston into a family of children's book artists, and had his first book, *Dinosaurs*, published at nineteen. Michael has spent the last thirty-five years travelling, writing and illustrating award-winning children's books while he figures out what he wants to do next. Michael lives in County Wicklow, Ireland.

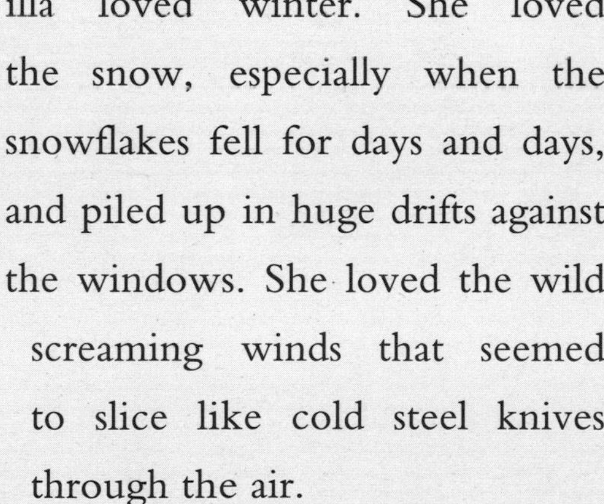

Silla loved winter. She loved the snow, especially when the snowflakes fell for days and days, and piled up in huge drifts against the windows. She loved the wild screaming winds that seemed to slice like cold steel knives through the air.

But most of all she loved the ice. For Silla was the Ice Queen.

She lived in an Ice Palace that had central freezing in every room, and microwave chillers where you could make your own instant ice cream. The curtains on the windows were made of chains of icicles that tinkled when you pulled them.

Silla loved to sit on her throne, looking out of the window at the dazzling white ice fields of her realm. Every day she drank a toast to the world of ice, from a cocktail glass full of chinking ice cubes, and sang a little song to herself:

"Ice is nice, ice is nice,
It grips your heart like a cosy vice,
I'd face any danger and I'd pay any price
For ice, ice, ice!"

When Silla wasn't at her window, she liked to sit in her cold tub, or snuggle down in her icy bed watching *Dancing on Ice* on the television.

Sometimes she went out and skated on the frozen lakes, or put on skis and zoomed down the mountain slopes. She would tour her land in a sleigh drawn by two very large emperor penguins, while her pet penguin, Pauline, sat beside her. Sometimes they had a picnic in a big cave, sheltered from the winds. They ate ice burgers and ice chips, and seven different kinds of ice cream. Then they would sit back happily and sing songs like 'Baby, It's Cold Outside' and 'Cool, Clear Water'.

One day, in the middle of one such song, Silla suddenly put her hand up and said, "Sssh!"

Pauline stopped singing and looked at Silla.

"Listen!" said the Ice Queen.

There was silence. Then they began to hear a regular sound, again and then again. It went on and on: *Plop! … Plop! … Plop! … Plop! …*

"Can you hear it, Pauline?"

Pauline nodded vigorously.

They listened again. The sound went on: *Plop! … Plop! … Plop! …*

Silla went to the mouth of the cave. On the ground they could see a small pool of water.

Into the pool, from an icicle on the cave roof, drops were falling, one by one.

Plop! … Plop! … Plop!

Pauline gazed at Silla. The Ice Queen looked alarmed.

"It's melting!" said Silla. "The icicle is melting!"

As they stared at the falling drops, they heard more plops start up. Another icicle on the roof was beginning to drip. Then another. And another. As more and more drops started falling around them, Silla and Pauline scooped up the remains of their picnic, and ran out into the open. The wind was blowing steadily, but Silla realised it was not the usual icy wind that she enjoyed so much. It was warm.

"A warm wind!" Silla was angry. "All things warm are banned from entering my domain! I won't allow it!"

Pauline the penguin shook her head, frowning.

"Where can it be coming from?" Silla wondered.

They both gazed around at the empty, icy land. Then Pauline gave a little squeak and pointed to the sky behind them with her left flipper.

Silla turned and looked. From beyond the distant slope above the cave, she could hear a faint chuckle of laughter. As she stared, the top of a head with tousled hair appeared slowly. The lips were pursed together, blowing out air down the mountainside.

Silla and Pauline could feel the warmth of the breath as the icicles continued to drip and drip.

The head rose further. It was ruddy and bearded, and the body attached to it followed. It was dressed in a long white robe, tied round the middle with a belt made of large seashells.

"How do you do?" came a voice from the luxurious beard. "My name is Zeffa, King of the

Warm Winds."

Silla, who had been standing still, speechless with rage, found her voice. "I don't care who you are!" she shouted. "You are invading my land. Go! Get out! NOW! Or I'll make sure there's not a warm breath left in your body!"

Zeffa held up his hand and said: "Peace! Lighten up, lady. I come in friendship."

Silla hissed with fury. "Friendship!" she shrieked. "You start melting my cave roof, and then talk about friendship? I said get out of here, now!"

"Keep your cool!" said Zeffa, smiling. He began to float slowly down the slope towards them.

"Stop right there!" shouted Silla, while Pauline peeped round from behind her and gave a yapping hiss of her own.

Zeffa took no notice, and kept floating towards them.

"I warned you!" snarled Silla. "I'll count to

three, then it's… ZAP!"

Still Zeffa continued floating in their direction.

Silla held her arms out in front of her. She knew her power. If she jabbed her arms forward, all her fingers pointing, whoever was in front of her would instantly freeze and turn into solid ice. This was how she had got rid of any of the early explorers she didn't like. Their frozen figures now decorated her sculpture garden.

As Zeffa gently came to land a few metres in front of them, Silla shouted: "Right, that's it! One! … Two! … Three! …"

She thrust her hands forward at him, her fingers spread out.

She waited. Nothing happened.

Zeffa smiled. He spread out his arms as if to say, *So what?*

Furiously the Ice Queen thrust her arms forward at him again. Once, twice, then a third time. Still there was no result.

"Don't waste your energy, my dear." Zeffa grinned. "It's no use. Like you, I am a being who lives in another, parallel world, immune to such spells and mumbo jumbo."

"Don't patronise me, you hairy joker!" snapped Silla. "I know your icicle-melting tricks are just the start. Soon you'll be roaming my land, breathing over the lakes and the ski slopes and the beautiful, glittering ice that I love and rule over. And before long they will all start to melt and disappear."

"Exactly! But let me explain. I want to make peace…"

"I don't want to hear any more!" said Silla. "This is war!"

"Very well," said Zeffa. "But I suggest, instead of sipping cocktails and singing songs and having picnics with your little friend, you go out and take a look at this land you say you rule so well. Take a good look, because it won't be here much longer; you have nearly lost the battle already. You might as well hear me out."

"Never!" said Silla. "This is war, not peace! All-out war!"

"All right," said Zeffa. "Catch me if you can!"

With a wave of his hand, the Ice Queen's enemy took a huge, deep breath, puffing out his great chest. Then he blew the air out all at once like a jet stream and propelled himself at enormous speed away across the icy wastes until he had disappeared from view over the far horizon.

Silla and Pauline stared after him, blinking in surprise.

"Enough!" snapped Silla. "It's time to rally

the troops. Pauline, sound the alert!"

Pauline gave a piercing cry that turned into a kind of wailing yodel that went on for several minutes.

From far and near came a flapping sound, and a chorus of squeaks and whistles, as crowds of penguins came out of their homes among the snows and gathered round the Ice Queen.

"Order, order!" said Silla. "Form ranks. On parade!"

The penguins began trying to obey, but they had no practice in drilling, so they just milled about, flapping at each other with their flippers in a vain attempt to line up.

"That will do," said Silla. "Well, comrades, there's no time to lose. Remember:

"Ice is nice, ice is nice!

Into battle, pay the price!

Ice, ice, ice, ice!"

The raggle-taggle troops didn't seem to be roused to much enthusiasm by this battle cry, but Silla climbed aboard her sleigh and gave an encouraging shout "Forward! Follow me! We shall beat that horrible hot-breathed hooligan!"

The Ice Queen surged ahead, her battalion of penguins following in a great unruly crowd, slithering and sliding and flapping their flippers. Silla felt that as a fierce military advance it wasn't very impressive. But she said nothing. At least she had her own powers to fall back on and if the worst came to the worst she could engage in a series of face-to-face personal combats with thc enemy.

When thcy *found* the enemy! That turned out not to be too easy.

The ramshackle procession went slithering and flapping, and padding and pawing its way towards the border of the Ice Queen's realm. When they got to Snowy Mountain, Silla looked puzzled and dismayed.

"Pauline," she said, "this is called Snowy Mountain, right?"

Pauline nodded her head firmly.

"Then where is the snow?"

Pauline looked around.

"It's gone!" cried the Ice Queen. "It must be that hot-air merchant Zeffa, breathing all over our mountains. I won't stand for it. Come on, troops, up and at 'em! We'll climb this peak and go down the glacier on the other side."

When they reached the top of the glacier, the Ice Queen cried, "Onward!" and with whoops of glee her battalion started to slide and slither down the gleaming slope of ice on the other side. The Ice Queen followed bumpily in her sleigh, but not far from the bottom the ice began to get soft and slushy, and before long it was more like a shallow river.

"He's been at it again!" roared Silla. "This glacier used to run right down as far as the sea. Before long he'll have it melted away. We've no time to lose. Keep going, it will be two hours before we reach shore."

The seashore marked the border of the Ice Queen's domain, where the ice ended and the ocean stretched out to the horizon.

Only ten minutes had passed when Pauline tapped Silla on the arm, and pointed ahead.

"Holy snowflakes!" cried Silla. "Stop the sleigh!"

Just a few metres in front of them, they could see the normally flat expanse of ice moving up and down slowly like an ocean swell. They could hear a creaking sound, as slabs of ice jostled with each other, and beyond that was the open sea. Huge flat chunks of ice that had broken off the mainland were floating in the water and, further out, icebergs rose up like giant white rocks from the water. The air was still and silent.

"This is terrible!" cried Silla. "My ice domain is shrinking. That foul fiend and his furnace breath is melting it away!"

The Ice Queen stepped down from her sleigh

and with Pauline beside her moved forward across the ice. Pauline handed her the binoculars she was carrying, and Silla gazed around. There was nothing to be seen.

"Come out, come out, wherever you are!" Silla shouted. Her voice carried across the empty landscape, and echoed among the mountains.

Suddenly they heard a loud CRACK! And then another, and another.

"Take cover!" cried Silla, as everyone crouched down. She looked around for their attacker, then Pauline began to squeak with alarm, and pointed back towards the land.

A gap had appeared in the ice. The slab they were on had broken off from the mainland and become an ice floe that was slowly floating away.

They rushed to the edge. The gap was too wide to jump. They were slowly floating away, out into the ocean.

Pauline spread her flippers and prepared to

dive. She looked over at Silla and beckoned encouragingly for her to follow.

"I can't swim," said Silla sadly. "I never needed to learn." A teardrop ran down her cheek and froze at once.

She and Pauline stood gazing at each other, perplexed.

A shout broke the silence. "Ahoy there, shipmates!"

They saw Zeffa, smiling broadly as he paddled a raft of ice towards them.

"Get back!" called Silla. "We are at war! I have brought my army to do battle with you and your cohorts!"

Zeffa went on paddling. "Yes, I see your army, and very terrifying they are..." He glanced towards the shore, where the bedraggled crowd of penguins stared out towards them. "But I have no cohorts. Look around. Not a single cohort in sight. I come alone, and I come in peace."

His raft was now right beside Silla's ice floe.

She knew her freezing powers were useless, so she simply glared at him while he stepped on to the floe, saying politely, "May I come aboard? I'd better help you get back to shore, before you drift away into the ocean. Then we can talk."

"I have nothing to say to you," said the Ice Queen haughtily. She turned her back on him and climbed into her sleigh. Pauline sat down beside her in support.

Zeffa smiled, and began to paddle.

When they were all safely back ashore, Zeffa said: "Now you see what we are up against. We need to fight this menace together."

"Together?" Silla was scornful. "You are the King of the Warm Winds. You hate the cold. Why would you want to save the ice?"

"The warming-up is worldwide. It's gone global. And that puts my land and my lifestyle in danger too."

"*Your* lifestyle? Surely the warmer the better

is your motto!"

"Listen to me, Silla. You love your chilly land, don't you? You love to lounge at your window with an iced drink in your hand and watch the snow fall and the gales blow cold winds. I have even heard that you sometimes have a bath in the kitchen freezer."

"How did you hear that?!" Silla snapped.

"I have my sources. But it's true, isn't it, that cold for you is just the ticket, the bees' knees, the icing on the cake…?"

"Cut the clichés, please. What's it to you, anyway?"

"Well, just as you like your icy life, I love to bask in the sun on tropical islands, sipping hot rum punch and blowing warm, balmy breezes to make the palm trees sway, and listening to the twang of guitars as the sunset glows like jewels on the ocean…"

"Sentimental claptrap!" Silla sneered.

"Maybe, but I love it just as much as you

love your shivery ways. And if we don't do something soon, we'll both be saying goodbye to it all for ever."

"But there are plenty of tropical isles for you to laze about on. What's the problem? I still think you've got some kind of trick up your sleeve."

"Come with me – I'll show you."

"Come where?"

"Take my hands, and hold on."

Reluctantly, Silla did so. Zeffa puffed out his chest and took a huge deep breath, as he had before. Then he blew it out with all his force.

"Hold on tight!" he cried, as the sleigh zoomed along like a plane on a runway, before taking off into the air.

Zeffa kept blowing with amazing strength, and before long Silla could feel the warmth of the tropical sun on her face. She shuddered.

"Look down," said Zeffa. "What do you see?"

"I see one of your tropical islands, and a bunch of those human creatures swarming around on the beaches. They have colonised the whole earth, those creepy-crawlies."

"Yes, and they'll finish it off, if we don't band together to stop them. Let us fly on a little way."

Soon they were flying high above the empty ocean, and Zeffa guided the sleigh down till they were hovering just above the water's surface.

"Now look down," said Zeffa. "This used to be onc of my favourite islands."

Below them, Silla could see the tops of palm trees poking out from the water, and here and there a tower and a steeple. She could vaguely make out some houses just below the surface too.

"Now you see why we are on the same side," said Zeffa. "If the world warms up any more, all your icy kingdom will melt, and the oceans will rise and rise, and not only will you lose your lands, but these islands will be drowned too, and all the forests and the deserts and the mountains. As well as all those hordes of humans in their tall cities where they live packed together like ants. It's their fault, you know."

"What is?"

"The drowning of the world. It's all down to them. Let me explain…"

"Do you mind if you do it back at my palace? I can't stand this heat much longer. I'm afraid I'm beginning to melt too."

"Certainly." Zeffa held her hands, then took a deep, deep breath and blew it out again with a roar.

Soon they were back in the Ice Queen's frosty land, where they got a great welcome from the assembled troops, who thought they had been abandoned. Then, together, they made the long trek home, the sleigh helped this time by several puffs from the king's amazing lungs.

He told Silla all about the warming of the world and the climate changes being caused by the polluting activities of the humans. He said that there were some humans who understood what was happening, and tried to campaign to stop it.

"We must help them," said Zeffa.

"But how?"

"We'll enlist your penguins. If they arrive wherever there are marches or demonstrations or scientists holding meetings to warn of the dangers, the publicity will be huge. Those humans just adore penguins – they think they're so cuddly and cute. If the humans think *they're* threatened, they may finally pay some attention."

"I'm sure it's worth a try," said Silla. She turned to Pauline. "You'll help us, won't you, Pauline?"

Pauline nodded and squeaked with enthusiasm.

"Then let's get busy. Pauline, you explain the plan, and we'll send you all out to campaign." Then, turning back to Zeffa, "But how will they get to these places?"

"That's my great idea – it will cause a sensation with those humans! The penguins will all swim together."

"But it's so far!"

"Don't forget the amazing power of my breath. I have made a study of global ocean currents. I'll plan their routes, get down just below the surface, and blow them along in the right direction. It will be the fastest sea travel ever."

"I wish I could help," said Silla, "but I get out of breath just climbing on to my throne."

"Walk along the shoreline," said Zeffa, "and keep doing your freezing trick as you go. It will stop some of the melting – for a while, anyway."

"I'll do it."

It took some time for Pauline to explain to the penguins just what she and Zeffa were hoping to do. Most of them were excited at the adventure – and even the lazier ones were persuaded, once they realised that all their homes, and even their lives, could be destroyed if they didn't get involved.

The next day the penguins assembled at the shore, and both Silla and Zeffa gave them a pep talk to tell them how they were helping to try to save the world and themselves from extinction.

Then Zeffa held out his hands, took a deep breath and called: "World Savers! Let's go swimming!"

There was a squeaking, growling, grunting cheer from the throng, and Zeffa led the penguins to the water's edge. In a mass of flapping flippers and waving paws they dived into the ocean, and at once became rulers of their own world, zipping along through the water with sleek speed.

Zeffa waved to Silla. "Farewell, friend!" he cried.

And Silla called back, "My friend, farewell and good luck!"

Zeffa plunged in.

Silla watched. She could see the penguins now and then leaping above the surface. Then she saw one penguin soar right out of the water, waving wildly. It was Pauline.

Silla waved and blew her a kiss, and Pauline dived back down into the ocean.

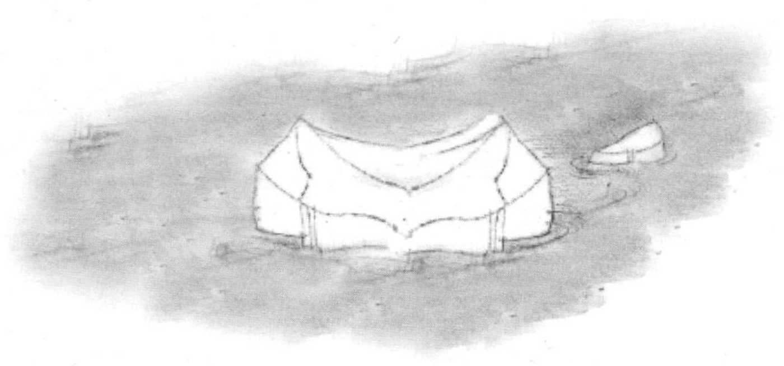

The Last Cat

Celine Kiernan

Illustrated by
Tatyana Feeney

Celine Kiernan is the author of The Moorehawke Trilogy, the first title of which, *The Poison Throne*, won the Readers' Association of Ireland Award for best book. Celine also wrote the multi-award-winning *Into the Grey*. She lives in rural Ireland where, despite being dyslexic, she writes about ghosts, talking animals and sometimes quite unpleasant things that go bump in the dark.

Tatyana Feeney is originally from North Carolina but now lives in Ireland. She has written and illustrated three picture books: *Small Bunny's Blue Blanket*, *Little Owl's Orange Scarf* and *Little Frog's Tadpole Trouble*. Tatyana has two lively and enthusiastic children and a small dog, who thinks he is a large dog.

I am not the one in need of playmates, you understand. The thought of children makes me shudder. Grabbish, clutching creatures with their love of tail pulling – most of them are beneath contempt.

No, I am not doing this for myself; I am doing it for the *girl*. She is the only reason for these foolish, nightly journeys out into the cold.

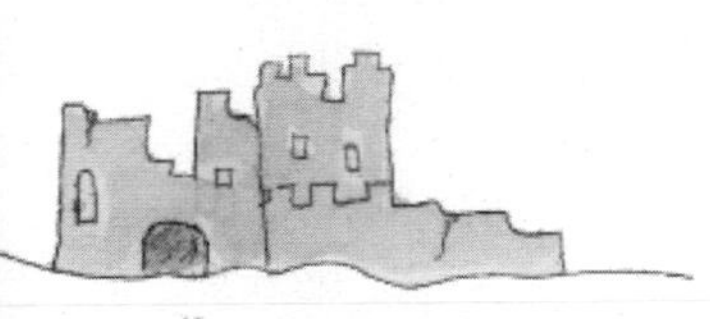

The king does not prevent my leaving, though I know he would prefer I stay. This does not surprise me. The man does nothing these days but sit and stare into the fire. His people come daily to his rooms, hoping to rouse him to action; have him roaring about the battlements, directing soldiers and firing cannon, as he used to only recently. But he has given up.

His lack of spirit frightens his people. Without him, they think they will lose the war. They are right, but I couldn't care less about their war. The king's lap is warm, and he is content for me to stay there as long as I wish – what more does a cat need from a man? Except perhaps a morsel or two to eat.

Slim chance of that these days.

The sun has been down for hours, and the air is chilly as I drop from the window on to the snow-muffled roof. Snow. Bah! No self-respecting cat with even half a brain goes out in snow if they can help it. It is already almost belly-deep as I pick my way along the parapets, and it is falling still, drifting like fat feathers from a starless sky. Those surfaces not snow-covered are already bitter with frost. I have left a warm fire and velvet-lined lap to be out here. I deserve a medal. Whatever a medal is. Something to be fondly wished for, if the soldiers are to be believed.

Mind you, I am sure I look very handsome – sleek and black against the white. Certainly I leave very pretty footprints. Perhaps snow is not *too* bad – aesthetically speaking, that is. The footprints will be useful – or I hope they will. I'm not certain what I will do if this latest attempt proves a failure.

The night is peaceful, with nothing to disturb its stillness but the *shush* and *hiss* of the waves at the base of the cliffs, and the whispering fall of snow.

The king's quarters are on the quiet side of the castle – its walls rising straight from the cliffs with nothing beneath them but a dizzying drop to the sea. Despite this, one can clearly hear the cannon fire and screaming that rises daily from the battlefield beyond the courtyards. The noise used to bother the girl. She used to cover her head with a pillow; her mother would encourage her to sing, and so they would attempt to defeat the cacophony of war with nothing but nursery rhymes and hymns. At such times, I was never certain which irritated me more: the soldiers' crashing about or the women's enthusiastic warbling. It was all enough to make one want to jump into the sea.

Ah well, such sounds have not troubled me for a while. These days all is stillness, even during daylight hours – stillness and listening, and besieged humans anxiously peering from watchtowers of burnt stone to the scattered flicker of the campfires on the other side. They are waiting for something; some great final moment that their enemies are constructing beyond the wall. The last explosive step in this hungry war. It will end them all. They are powerless to stop it.

I could walk round the battlements, if I chose, and reach the front of the castle that way. The sentries used to like me to do so. "*Féach!*" they would say. "*Caitín an bhanprionsa.*" "Look! The princess's little cat." Even during battle my presence used to cheer them. I have had soldiers pet me and croon to me even as they hid from rains of arrows. I have had them share their hasty dinners, gently offering scraps of meat with fingers stained with human blood. There have been no dinners for many a day now, and the soldiers have grown less than kind. So I no longer bother with them. Instead, I pick my way across the moon-bright roof, heading for the broken wall that will be my stairway to the ground; its tumbled stones make a convenient shortcut down into the courtyard.

There is much rubble down here now. It

makes getting from place to place an interesting experience. For a while, rats abounded, sneaking and skittering about within the debris. I quite like the occasional rat. They are fun to fight and are very tasty. But the humans have long since eaten every one.

Selfish creatures.

Through the bombed-out tennis courts I go, across the ruined chapel, and up to the top of the graveyard wall. Everything here is fattened by the snow; the tall grave-markers and the flat-topped crypts. Even the stone angels are gentled by it, their outflung wings made soft and softer still as the great white flakes sift down.

Within the graveyard the girl is playing tennis. She has only one racquet these days and no partner to play with, so she hits the ball again and again against the graveyard wall. Even to my sensitive ears, the *toc, toc, toc* of ball against stone is barely audible. Even to me it is a lonely sound. I meow, hoping the girl will look up.

But she does not.

She is the last remaining child. After the bombing, the king had all the others lowered down the cliffs in baskets, and taken in boats to who knows where. I was not sorry to see them go, of course, but I do feel a certain pang for the girl. She always enjoyed other children's company, and…

Bah. This is pure foolishness. Even had they stayed, they would have been of no use to her. Not now. Still. I should like the girl to be a little more cheerful. I meow again, quietly this time, as I gaze down at her, then I continue my journey onwards.

The girl's mother is seated on a stone bench at the corner of the graveyard. She is, as always, staring up at the tower where her husband sits – both of them waiting in vain for the other to visit. But he cannot see her; she cannot see him. What possible use are they to each other now? She is nothing but a glimmer within the ivy-clad shadows as I trot unseen above her. At the end of the wall I glance back, but of course neither mother nor girl is aware of my presence. As I slip down between the stones the sound of the girl's game follows me. She will play all night, as the mother will sit all night, soft shimmers among the graves until the morning sun erases them.

The king thinks that every possible hole and crevasse in his great castle has been blocked against the threat of invasion. This may be so if one is *human*. But I am a cat. I come and go as I please. I creep into the narrow places, the tunnels and culverts that exist unseen and mostly forgotten beneath the heavy castle walls.

Under the moat I go, through seeping darkness that is almost impenetrable even to my eyes. Within moments, I emerge into the crystalline beauty of an open field of snow. Once again, I am struck with the freshness of the air outside the castle walls. I pause to breathe it in. There is no smell of blood or human terror here. There is only the bright clarity of the moon, and the snow falling to blanket the dead and pillow the edges of shattered war machines.

I cross the treacherous stretch of ground that humans call 'no-man's-land'. The footprints I leave on the snow's new surface are sharp and clear; they mark an unmistakable path leading back the way I've come.

Surely he cannot fail to see it this time?

The air remains fresh for only a while; then I am within the enemy camp. It stinks as badly here as it does inside the castle. War has such a putrid smell; there is nothing natural to it at all. I know I am not safe here. On a previous visit,

I was almost caught – by a snare, if you can believe my being so stupid; a vicious loop of wire that closed about my neck and from which I barely escaped. I would have ended up in some soldier's stew pot, I have no doubt. Or roasting on a spit above a sputtering fire. The humans here are no better off for meat than those inside the castle walls, and cat meat is as tasty as any when a soldier's belly is stuck to his backbone. So I avoid the pools of orange firelight and, slinking between the icicle-hung tents, I stay outside the radius of murmured conversations until I get to the boy.

He is as I have found him every night – hunched in the corner of a ramshackle tent, trying to clean the rust from a pile of discarded armour. He does not notice the snow drifting in through the ragged walls. He does not notice the splintered table or leaning tent poles, or the air of lonely isolation that hangs about this bombed-out place. He only notices the pile of armour and how rusted it is. He only knows how badly he needs to clean it. The man who owns this armour is a bully – worse, he is a coward – and therefore much inclined to prove his strength by hurting those smaller than he. The boy is frightened to stop his work. If he cannot clean these pieces of metal – these meaningless pieces of metal – he knows the man will beat him.

I pick my way through the debris to sit by the boy's feet. He stays hunched over the armour, rubbing and rubbing at rust that will never go away. The man who owns this armour cannot hurt him any more – the boy has moved far beyond his reach – but I do not know how to tell him this. I meow but, like my girl, the boy does not look up.

I bat the snow that is falling unheeded by his side.

I jump to and fro in the drifts that have piled against the armour.

Look! Look! See?

I huff and tussle and throw great showers of snow into the air. I roll and yowl and scuffle up its pristine surface in a wanton luxury of destruction. For a moment, I forget what it is I am trying to do and simply enjoy myself. Then I catch a glimpse of the boy's expression, and stop. I sit up in the mess of snow and stare into his dirty heedless face, which is only inches from mine, as he continues to scour and scour and never look up.

Over the last couple of nights, I've tried everything a cat can think of to make this boy see me. I've meowed. I've hissed. I rubbed myself against him. I even laid myself atop his work – quite literally draping my body across the armour over which he hunches – hoping it would force him to stop. This tactic has never failed me in the past. I once disrupted a council of war in exactly such a manner! But all this hollow-cheeked little urchin did was spit once again on to his ragged sleeve and turn his attention to another spot.

The indignity.

I almost left him there and then, I tell you. I almost abandoned both of them – him *and* the girl – and stalked out into the night as the rest of the palace cats have done, away from this horrible place and the horrible smell of horrible humans hating and dying and setting things afire.

Almost, I say. Almost. But not quite.

What stopped me leaving? I don't know… a strange thing… a little thing… a feeling.

It is hard to explain.

Something happened inside my chest that day when the bomb fell on to the tennis courts. I looked at the piles of smoking rubble where the girl and her mother had only just been standing, and it felt as if something had cracked inside me or… or as if something *broke*. All I know is that it happened when I thought the girl was gone from me; a nasty feeling that I had never experienced before. I do not *like* this feeling. I do not want to keep experiencing it – but it seems to live in my chest now. Each time she looks at me and cannot see me, it gets bigger.

I am angry now, thinking about it, and I prowl to the door of the tent in frustration and sit down in the snow. Behind me the boy scours and scours as if his life depends on it, and I think of my girl, hitting a solitary ball against a heedless wall. I am so lonely I could weep.

She fed me from a pipette of milk when I was a kit. She used to carry me in her pocket. Later, when I was too haughty to allow this kind of affection, I would follow her, as if by accident, and sleep in nearby patches of sunshine while she did her lessons or read or climbed trees. She was a demon for tree-climbing. Sometimes I would join her up there in the branches; we would grin into the breeze together high above the ground.

My first memory is of her. It is not a good

one. I was very young, my siblings and I still nothing but milk-addled balls of fur. We barely understood what was happening when those children came and took us from the hay. I heard my mother yowling as they put us in the sack. I heard the children yelling, and singing *ding dong dell…* and then all was bubbling water and no air as my brothers and I scratched and tore each other, trying to escape the darkness and cold as the river they had thrown us into closed the sack tight around us.

Hers was the first face I saw when the neck of the sack opened to sunshine and air. She was soaking wet from having jumped in the water. My brothers were cold around me, and her hands were only marginally warmer as she lifted me from their motionless tangle.

"*Oh…*" she said. "*Féach, níl ach ceann amhain beo.*"

"There's not but one of them alive."

I close my eyes and sink my head on to my

forepaws. The snow kisses my ears and shoulders and the back of my neck as I ask myself, *Why?* Why didn't I love her more openly? Why didn't I kiss her every minute of every day she was alive? Why didn't I sleep, like the faithful friend I should have been, round her shoulders and allow her to scratch my ears and stroke my back the way I know she would have loved.

I miss you. I miss you, my princess. I want you back.

"*Tá sé ag cur sneachta.*"

I glare round at the boy. He is gazing up in wonder as the snow falls thick and heavy through a hole in the tent roof above him.

Yes, I sneer, *it is snowing. Now tell me something I do not already know.*

He is delighted and sticks out his tongue to try to catch a snowflake.

Oh! I get to my feet, realising. He sees it. The boy *sees* it! I knew he would! When the snow first started to fall I saw the girl pause – just for a fraction of a moment – to watch the bright flakes drift from the darkness of the sky. I knew then this would be my chance.

Hey! Hey, boy! Over here! Look at me!

I back out of the tent. I leap and I tumble. I scurry and dodge. I whisk great tailfuls of snow into the air.

The boy peers in my direction – not quite certain. Then he laughs, and he is up and following me, lost in the delicious puzzlement of what is happening to the snow. He looks just like a boy again – like a boy on an adventure. He has forgotten his master; he has forgotten to be afraid. Looking up into his face I imagine that this boy would very much enjoy climbing trees.

The men are dragging cannon through the snow as we make our way through camp. They are cold and miserable, and they are trying very hard not to make any noise. They cannot see the boy at all and they are too busy to notice me. At least I hope they are too busy. I confess that I am frightened as they move around us in the dark. I do not want these men to notice me.

The boy is all aglow with wonder and delight, his smile as bright as the moon. His was the face that hovered over me while I choked and strangled at the end of that lethal piece of wire. His were the shaking fingers that released me from the snare. He shooed me into the night, then stood to face the bellowing man who had seen him free me. Last I saw was his skinny body stepping between me and my pursuer, the man's fist raised against the firelight, ready to strike. I heard the boy cry out, and I fled.

I look up into his face again, and I realise I'm not just doing this for the girl.

An eye for an eye, I think, *a tooth for a tooth*. A friend for a friend.

I lead him across the snow and moonlight,

away from the soldiers who are lining up cannon in the dark.

At the castle wall, I squeeze between the stones into a crack barely wide enough to allow the passage of a rat, let alone a cat. The boy follows me with ease. His presence illuminates the darkness as brightly as any moon. I feel him grinning in excitement as he follows me through the dark. I don't think he sees me – not really – but he knows there's something good ahead of him: something better than a rusty pile of armour and the threat of an angry fist.

We emerge next to the ruined fountain. He scrambles behind me across tumbled stone and fallen timber as I lead him to the small door at the base of the graveyard wall. The *toc, toc, toc* of the girl's game halts when we step inside. I weave and flow round the boy's ankles as he pauses shyly at the threshold. Of course, no one sees me; all eyes are on the boy. The girl steps forward, the ball forgotten in her hand. Her mother rises to her feet. From her corner of shadows, she recognises what the girl does not: that this is a foreigner; that this is one of *them*.

The girl discards her solitary racquet. With a laugh, she throws the ball. It is a good throw – the boy has to dodge the gravestones to catch it. He aims, and fakes a throw. Together they laugh as she leaps for empty air.

He throws. She catches. She throws. Their laughter is as gentle as the moonlight. At the sound of it, the mother sits back down. I make my way round to her side, and curl beneath the ivy there, watching the children play their game. The sun will come up soon, and with it will come the bombs and the fighting. The war will end today. I doubt there will be much left standing when it is done.

I suppose it would be wise for me to run. I think instead I will stay right where I am.

I close my eyes. I might sleep for a while. Beyond the castle walls, men are preparing cannon, but in this graveyard I can hear children playing. I am content even as the sun comes up and the bombs begin to fall. I am content even as the world falls down around me. No matter what happens, I know that right here a young girl and a young boy are throwing a ball to each other and laughing. I know their game will continue for ever. I hope that when I awake, they will see me at last.

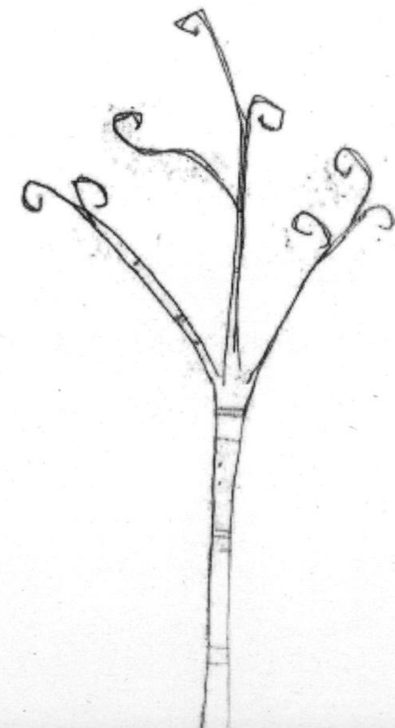

Across the Cold Ground

OISÍN MCGANN

Illustrated by Oisín McGann

Oisín McGann has written and illustrated numerous books for all ages, including the surveillance state thriller, *Rat Runner*, and the steampunk series, The Wildenstern Saga. He is a winner of the Bisto/CBI Book of the Year Merit Award and has been shortlisted for a number of others, including the Waterstones Children's Book Prize in the UK, le Grand Prix de l'Imaginaire in France and Locus Magazine's Best First Novel Award in the US. Oisín lives in the Irish countryside, where he won't be heard shouting at his computer.

When he was a boy, Charley dreamed of war – of being a soldier, a warrior, a hero. Back then, he never thought it would involve so much *digging*. In the chilly gloom of the swampy trench,

the sergeant urged them on, growling quietly through gritted teeth.

"Come on now, lads! Dig! Clear it out before the next lot comes down on us! Dig, if you want to live, you little beauties. Dig if you want to live!"

Charley's cold, numb fingers gripped the short handle of the spade. His body ached, weak with exhaustion. The spade's handle was slippery with mud, and he lost his hold on it every now and again. It was all the more dangerous because he'd sharpened the blade too, because he needed to use it as a weapon sometimes. So he'd come close to cutting a gash in his leg more than once as it slipped in his hands.

"That could have been us, under there," Mick said, working beside him. "We could've been buried under there, you and me."

Mick was Charley's best mate. They had enlisted together, trained together. They'd been sent out on to this insane battlefield in France together. They shared a dug-out together. Now that dug-out was buried here under tons of earth.

"Yeah, well we weren't," Charley replied. "Just lucky, I suppose."

"Quit that chatter!" the sarge rasped.

It was dark, and the small group of men and everything around them was *cold*. Charley was cold to his bones, like he'd never be warm again. A light shower of snow had fallen that day, on the hard, frozen ground. The floor of the trench was still like a marsh, though. It always was, its surface beaten soft by the constant traffic of boots.

The steam of Charley's breath looked bright in the darkness. At least the digging was getting him moving. They worked by the light of the stars in the clear night sky. The front wall of their part of the trench, eight feet high, had collapsed during the last German bombardment. Now they were struggling to get the mass of chalky clay dug out and the wall repaired before the German gunners dropped any more shells on them.

Snow was falling again, and he looked up into the sky to see it shower out of the darkness towards him. They were working in the dark because, with the wall collapsed, the ramp of earth offered little protection. German snipers, crack shots, waited for an opportunity to pick off anyone who raised their head too high.

Then there was the artillery. Charley had been terrified of it since he'd first heard the blasts, felt the first impacts through the ground only weeks before. There was nothing you could do to stay safe during the bombardments. You just cowered there against the wall of your dug-out, curling yourself into whatever cover you could find. You clutched your helmet to your head, scared as a child, as explosions punched craters in the earth around you. Sometimes they got so close, the noise of the explosions was like someone stamping on your brain. All you could do was hope and pray there wasn't a shell plummeting right down on your position. You could only wait to see if it was your turn to be killed by the blast or the shrapnel.

"Agh! Oh, for the love o' God!"

Mick was hopping around, a grimace on his face. The muck they were standing in was too thick and deep to hop around in, and he nearly fell over as his boot got stuck.

"Don't tell me you hit your foot *again*?" Charley laughed at him. "What kind of eejit are you? Keep it up, Mick, and you'll end up chopping your toes off all together."

"Grand," Mick grunted. "Maybe the brass will send me home."

"They don't let you out of the war for chopping off your toes. They're wise to that kind of stuff. They'll just shoot you for bein' a chancer!"

"Well, they may come down and do some

diggin' themselves so," Mick retorted. "Better yet, let them come and get shelled! See how long they last before they start thinking about losing some toes an' all."

Charley nodded, snorting.

"All right, so I've got a sore foot," Mick said. "Still, you're the bigger eejit. Leavin' your gloves in the dug-out like that in this cold. Three of the lads are down with frostbite, Charley! Pat lost four fingers! I'd rather lose my toes to a spade than my fingers to the cold."

This was their thing when they were bored – playing "Who's the Bigger Eejit?", a game that could go on for hours sometimes. Or until one of the other soldiers snarled that, by the holy Mary, they'd better shut up or he'd shoot them before the Germans got the chance.

Somewhere under all that pulverised clay was the hole burrowed in the ground where they normally ate and slept. Half their kit was buried in there too. They'd both been in the latrine when the bombardment started. They'd brought their rifles with them because the sarge would have their heads if they went anywhere without their weapons. But apart from that, they only had whatever they carried on their belts or in their coat pockets. The artillery shell had landed on their dug-out while they were relieving themselves a mere forty yards away.

"Less talking, more digging!" the sarge's voice barked softly in the darkness. "My word, who'd be daft enough to have Irishmen in the army?"

"British officers, Sarge," Charley replied, and Mick giggled.

"Less of that cheek!" came the throaty growl. "Dig, my lovely lads. Build us a nice strong house, before the wolf comes huffin' and puffin' again."

The sarge was all right. He was British Army, through and through, and was forever cracking Irish and Scottish jokes, but he was the first you'd go to for help. Like an angry dad, he was always giving out, but he looked out for his boys too. The men of Charley and Mick's company were mostly Irish, but they trusted their English sergeant – far more than they did the officers anyway. He was always there with them. Always first over the top ahead of them.

"Post!" someone called down the line. "The post is here!"

"Ah, here." Mick paused as he was about to toss away another clod of clay. "They never send us post when we're on the front line. Something's up."

"We go over the top in the morning," Charley said. "They're tryin' to boost morale."

"They want to boost my morale? Tell me I'm not goin' over the top."

"It's what we're here to do, Mick. You're the eejit for enlisting."

"Yeah, right. But at least I was the eejit who knew what he was enlisting *for*. You joined the *army* to find your *brother*. Did you not know there was a *war* on?"

"Ah, leave off, will ya?" Charley snapped at him, feeling suddenly angry.

Throwing down his spade, he cursed and kicked at a sod of mud. He was still standing there, blowing on his freezing hands and trying to stop his teeth from chattering, when he heard his name shouted.

"Charley Burn? Charley! Post for you, mate!"

He turned too suddenly, finding his feet held tight by the sucking mud. Losing his balance, he toppled over into the massive puddle behind him with an almighty splash. The water was icy cold, shocking the breath from his lungs. The others burst out laughing, but the sarge roared at them to shut up.

"Burn! Get yourself out of there, you fool! I swear, it's like dealing with children! Get those clothes off you and get dry before you freeze to death!"

Mick helped haul him out, and Charley stood there sourly, trying to scrape the worst of the dirt off. There was nowhere to wash in the trenches, and no hope of getting his uniform clean before they went into action in the morning. And any spare clothes he had were buried in the dug-out.

"Go and get yourself sorted out," Mick told him. "I'll get your post."

Shivering with the cold, humiliated and miserable, Charley went off in search of a blanket, and a fire to dry his clothes.

Sitting in another dug-out, wrapped in someone else's blanket, Charley clutched a mug of hot tea. He stared into the fire burning in the brazier in front of him. He was warm enough, but he knew his uniform tunic and trousers probably wouldn't be dry by morning. His coat *definitely* wouldn't be dry. When dawn came, he'd have to put on his wet clothes and march out into the cold.

As he had done so many times before, he cursed his rotten luck. He wasn't supposed to be here. He'd just come looking for his older brother, Will, who'd joined the army before the start of the war. Sitting huddled as close to the fire as he could get, trying to soak up the warmth into his shivering body, he remembered sitting in the kitchen at home in Dublin. He was drinking tea then too – except that back then, there'd been milk and sugar. His mother went to answer a knock at the front door and came in carrying a telegram from the War Office. Will had been serving in France, and every soldier's family dreaded receiving one of those telegrams.

She couldn't bear to read it, handing it to Charley instead. But it didn't say Will was dead. It said he was missing in action. Charley's ma had broken down in tears, sobbing in hoarse cries as he read out the words, but Charley wouldn't give up hope. 'Missing' wasn't 'dead'. Will could still be alive.

Charley had enlisted the very next day, determined to find his brother. And Mick had come with him, saying he was going that way anyhow.

Of course, they'd known next to nothing about the army, and how it worked. Charley was never given a chance to search for his brother, and was shipped straight to France after training. He shook his head at the memory, and tried to scrape more of the drying clay from his hands and arms.

Mick ducked his head as he came in through the timber-framed entrance of the dug-out. It was little more than a large hole in the ground, big enough to hold three or four men if they squeezed in. The walls and roof were shored up with planks of wood and bags of clay, just like the walls of the trenches themselves.

"Here you go," Mick said. "You got

chocolate. I gave the lads theirs."

Charley scowled and rolled his eyes. They always showed each other what they got in their parcels from home, but Mick tended to open Charley's post as if it were his own. Which was annoying, to say the least. And whenever anyone in the trench got chocolate, they shared it round. It was just what everyone did.

"That was nice of you," Charley said grimly, "but I'd prefer to open my own post if you don't mind."

"How could you? You're covered in muck!"

"It's still *my post*. I hope you left me a decent piece of the chocolate!"

"Of course I did – you got the biggest bit!"

Mick held up the remains of the packet of Cadbury's chocolate. There was a letter with it. Charley frowned, not recognising the handwriting. The envelope had been opened too.

"Mick!"

"I didn't do that – it was open already. Your mother sent it in a parcel with the chocolate."

"Is that all there was?"

"Yeah, it's odd, isn't it? She normally puts in more stuff than that. Are you going to read the letter?"

"My hands are filthy. Stick it in with my first-aid kit – that pocket's still dry. I'll read it later. On my own."

"All right, don't be so touchy. Are you going to eat your chocolate now?"

"No, I'll keep that till later too. To have with my letter."

A letter from home was a precious thing. Charley wanted to wait until he could read it in comfort... and in some peace and quiet. A letter and some chocolate was an experience to be savoured.

"What 'later', you eejit?" Mick asked in exasperation, putting the chocolate down on the wooden crate that served as a table in the dug-out. "We all ate ours right up! We go *over the top* in a few hours. There might not *be* a later."

"That's a fine way to talk. I'm not about to— Mick! MICK! Watch out!"

As Mick was placing the letter in the inside pocket of Charley's jacket, a rat the size of a small cat jumped up on to the crate and grabbed the crumpled packet of chocolate. With a cry of horror, Charley lunged up from his seat, but the rat was already bolting out through the doorway. Mick swore loudly and scrambled out after it.

Still dressed in nothing but his long-johns underwear, Charley threw off the blanket, shoved his bare feet into his squelchy boots, and rushed out into the horrible, biting cold. The rat was making off along the trench with Mick sprinting after it, yelling at the men ahead to stop it. A chorus of

shouts rose up as the alarm was raised.

"The rat, stop the rat!"

"What's going on?"

"That rat's got Charley's chocolate!"

"The little maggot! Look! There it goes!"

"Kill it! Somebody shoot the bleedin' thing!"

They all gave chase, swearing and cheering. The rat scampered over the mud while the soldiers stamped and slid around it. Planks had been used to cross the bigger, ice-encrusted puddles, but it was still hard work running through the mire that carpeted the trench. And the light fall of snow had been reduced to slush underfoot. There were few lights too, which made things even more difficult.

The men charged about, desperately trying to stop the rat, but it evaded them all. Charley whimpered in despair as the creature scampered up the stack of clay bags that supported a section of the eight-foot-high wall. It raced out through the barbed wire and disappeared into the darkness of no-man's-land between the British trench and the German positions.

No one followed it out there. Not for a bit of chocolate. Not a chance.

"Sorry, Charley," Mick said. "I'm really sorry. Sure you wouldn't have wanted it anyway, would you? After it had been in the rat's mouth?"

The lads turned and headed back to their dug-outs, some of them patting Charley's back or squeezing his arm in sympathy. Mick pulled off his jacket and threw it over Charley's shivering shoulders.

"Come on, mate," he said. "You'll catch your death coming out dressed like that. Let's get you warm."

"Ah, Mick," Charley moaned, as he allowed his friend to lead him back down the trench. "My chocolate, Mick! The little devil stole my chocolate!"

"I know, mate. It was my fault."

"You're too right it was! If we make it through tomorrow, you'll owe me some bloomin' chocolate, Mick!"

"I know it. I'm so sorry, Charley."

As he stood listening to the distant booms and thuds of their artillery shelling the German lines, Charley shifted his shoulders uncomfortably in his damp woollen tunic. His uniform was heavier and stiff from its soaking, and still not properly dry. He had his helmet on, but he wasn't wearing his coat. It was too bulky, and it was still wet anyway. He couldn't get warm. The weak morning sun was doing little to help. All of the men in his company were standing in lines near the ladders and steps that led out of the trench, waiting for the order to advance.

He wished he'd kept hold of his gloves – his fingers were sore from the terrible chill in the air. The rifle was cold and hard and heavy. Leaning it against the clay bags, he stuck his hands into his armpits to try and get some movement back in his fingers. At the sergeant's order, all the men fixed bayonets, the familiar swarm of clicks carrying down the trench as they attached the long knives to the ends of the barrels of their Lee Enfield rifles. Charley readied his own weapon and stamped his feet in his damp boots, trying to work some warmth into his feet.

He was shivering. It could have just been the cold, or it could have been because of what was about to happen. *Don't think*, he told himself. Don't think. Don't think. Thinking'll just scare you. Just get out there and keep up with the lads. The artillery seemed to be further away now. That was how it would be. The shelling would creep forward over the German positions, and Charley and the others would get up out of the trench and follow the rain of bombs across the trail of devastation left behind.

He was weighed down with all the kit he had to carry on his webbing. Most of it was borrowed, because he'd lost so much when his dug-out was buried. There was a lot he had to bring with him, and it would slow him down, make it so hard to walk through the swamp out there.

His thoughts drifted to the letter tucked into the inner pocket of his tunic. It hadn't occurred to him, but it could have been word about Will. Perhaps he should have read it, instead of keeping it for later. Mick could be right. There might not be a 'later'.

"You'll stay beside me, won't you, Mick?" Charley asked in a tense voice.

"Of course I will, Charley. Sure, where else would I be?"

Then the lieutenant blew the whistle, and the sarge was the first up the ladder, leading the men out of the trench. Charley's hands were shaking as he slung his rifle on to his shoulder and took hold of the ladder.

Don't think. Get up that ladder. Just get out

there and keep up with the lads.

And a moment later, he was over the top, head down, working his way carefully through the coiled lines of barbed wire into the murky hell of no-man's-land. Smoke drifted over the landscape like a fog, making the place feel like something from a ghost story. There had been fields and woods here once. Now it was churned-up earth and shattered tree stumps. Frosty, crusted earth, with troughs and shell craters full of icy water. Parts of it frozen solid, other parts treacherously soft. The snow made everything look black and white. With the heavy kit hanging off him, every footstep through the muddy snow took effort.

The men spread out, and soon Charley found it hard to see the others around him through the murk. The whistling and crashing of the artillery was still close enough to drown out most sounds, but he could hear the clatter of machine guns and the bee-like whine of bullets shooting past. Mick was close by, and they both staggered on through the muck, their fear climbing over them as they drew closer and closer to where they knew the first German trench would be.

They kept their heads down and kept walking, their rifles held in front of them. Shells started falling closer. They still couldn't see much through the pall of smoke, but some of the explosions went off close enough for the two lads to feel the whump of the blasts through the air. This couldn't be their own guns – it had to be German artillery, aimed at the advancing British forces.

Charley tried to think of nothing. He kept his head down and kept walking. Bullets cut the air around him. The shells exploded ever closer. Then he was stumbling through the stretches of barbed wire in front of the German trench.

He crouched down, taking out his cutters. Mick held the tangled wire as Charley snipped his way through. It took time. The shells were deafening as they burst the earth around the two young soldiers, but the smoke was working in their favour. They couldn't see the Germans, but the enemy couldn't see them either.

"The machine guns are nowhere near us," Mick shouted over the noise, wincing as dirt showered down on them from a nearby blast. "There must be none in this part of the trench!"

Charley nodded. They were finally through the last stretch of wire. With their rifles levelled before them, they jumped up and ran full tilt through the fug of smoke at the German trench, screaming like animals to try and unnerve the men they were coming to kill. Charley got there first, trying to stop before he went over the edge, but slipping in the snow-covered mud. He lost his helmet as he skidded on to his backside and slid feet-first over the lip of the trench.

It was a long drop, and he landed badly, overloaded with heavy kit. He cried out as his ankle twisted painfully, but was up in a crouch in an instant, rifle raised, aiming one way, then the other. Mick came crashing down beside him, cursing loudly. Moments later, he too was up on one knee, rifle at the ready.

The trench was empty. It seemed slightly quieter here too than it was up top. The explosions sounded further away, and the smoke gave the place a haunted feel. They waited there, back to back, their breath pluming in the cold air. They waited for the enemy soldiers they *knew* must be here. The protective walls were destroyed in places, but the trench had survived the bombardment remarkably well.

"This is a good trench," Charley said, looking up at the walls. "Deeper than ours. Better supports too."

"Aye," Mick replied. "What's goin' on,

Charley? Where is everybody?"

"Don't know. Didn't see any sign of the lads coming through the wire."

"No sign of the *Germans* either. Here, we 'aven't got lost, have we?"

"No. This is the place."

They walked carefully along the trench, rifles still raised. Charley was limping on his injured ankle. There was no one here – no enemy, nor any of their own lads. It was much like their own trench, with dug-outs and reinforced walls. Scraps of uneaten food and empty tins lay around, as well as discarded equipment, as if the Germans had left in a hurry. There was the odd helmet or box of ammunition, a split boot and a tin opener. But no soldiers to defend the place.

They came to a part of the trench that had collapsed completely. They couldn't see how much of it was damaged. They'd have to climb up and crawl to find the rest of the network. Up into the machine-gun fire and the exploding shells. They turned and went back the other way. Less than fifty yards in the other direction; that end had been destroyed too. The only way out was up on to the battlefield.

"So... we've taken the place we were supposed to take," Mick exclaimed. "The Germans must have pulled back before we even got here, cos of the bombardment. What are we going to do now?"

"Shelling sounds like it's easing up," Charley said, rubbing his hand through his hair, wishing he hadn't lost his helmet. "We should head out one end or the other, try and hook up with some of the other lads, wherever they are. I don't want to be caught here on our own if the Germans come looking for their trench back."

"Here, Charley, you're bleeding. You've got blood on your head."

Charley looked at his hand, and saw blood on it. He touched the cut on his scalp. It was long, but shallow. He'd probably scraped his head on some wire or something when he fell. Just another thing to add to his list of mishaps over the last day and night.

Taking his first-aid kit from the inner pocket of his tunic, he opened the tin box, pulled out one of the dressings and pressed the pad against the cut while Mick tied the bandage round his head. Charley put the box away in his pocket and buttoned up his tunic.

"Right then," Mick said. "Let's get going."

They scrambled up the pile of frosted muck until they were out on the battlefield once more. There was still shelling going on, but it was quieter and more distant, and the machine-gun fire had thinned out. This time however, the pair didn't walk. Keeping close to the ground, they began to crawl along the crater-strewn earth towards where they thought the rest of the trench was, fervently hoping their men had captured it.

They'd gone about fifteen yards when, on

impulse, Charley checked his tunic, suddenly remembering his letter.

It was gone. His heart thumped against his chest.

"Mick!" he called quietly. "Mick, hang on! Mick! Hold on there, I've lost my letter!"

Mick looked back, frustration on his face, but he turned round too and followed Charley as he started back towards the trench they'd just left. A letter from home was a precious thing. Charley knew what had happened. It had been in the pocket with his first-aid kit. When he'd pulled out the kit, the letter must have come out with it and fallen to the ground. He reached the trench and slid down the ramp of earth, looking around until he saw the pale rectangle of the envelope in the mud.

"Got it!" he shouted, spinning to look up at his friend who was rising from a crouch to walk down the pile of earth into the trench.

Just at that moment, there came that hated

whistling sound and all hell erupted. A barrage of shells exploded across the ground in quick succession. Mick was thrown forward into the trench, landing face down in the mud. Charley shoved the letter into a pocket and rushed forward, but Mick was already lifting himself up. He was hurt, there was blood on the back of his right leg. Charley hauled him into a dug-out, shielding him as best he could with his own body.

"Well, this... is... is a f-f-f-fine state... state of affairs!" Mick groaned through clenched teeth.

He went to say something else, but drew in a sharp breath as the pain in his leg shut him up. Charley tore open the fabric of his friend's trousers to examine the wound. Instead of a single large one, he saw a dozen smaller shrapnel wounds down the back of Mick's thigh. None of them were too serious on their own, but together they'd lose a lot of blood, and the first-aid dressings he and Mick had wouldn't cover them all. Still, he bound them up as best he could, then held his friend against him as they tried to bear the pounding explosions that shook the earth around them.

Mick's face was pale, but he was still conscious. The explosions began to move away from the trench, chewing up the earth of no-man's-land. Charley raised his head to check the wounds again. They were still bleeding. Charley swore under his breath. Mick needed proper medical help. If the wound didn't kill him, infection or just the freezing cold would finish him before long. But there was nowhere they could go. The only help lay back in the British trenches. He'd have to carry his friend on a bad ankle, through the jaws of the bombardment.

"Read the... the letter," Mick said, shivering.

"What?"

"It saved our lives, Charley. We'd have been up there in the open when those shells landed, if you hadn't dropped that letter. You *saved* us, you eejit. Read the letter. It's not like we can go anywhere, can we? What else have we got to pass the time?"

Charley sighed and wiped his hands clean as best he could. Then he pulled the envelope out. It was dirty and crumpled now. He looked again at the handwriting, but couldn't identify it. Opening the envelope, he drew out the letter. It was short, written on a single sheet of paper. He frowned when he looked at the name and address written on the top. It only took moments to read the first few lines to himself, and a sob escaped from his throat.

"Charley? What is it, lad? Read it out, for God's sake!"

Charley held his hand out in front of Mick, who clutched it in his own.

"It's from an Oberleutnant Karl Ehrlichmann," Charley began. "At an address in Hamburg, Germany. It says: "Dear Mrs Burn, I hope you will forgive me for being the bearer of bad news, and for taking so long to deliver it. I am terribly sorry to inform you that your son, William, died in action on the first of July, 1916. As you will learn from reading this, I knew your son only briefly, but I am the only person who can pass on his last words, and so I must.

"I was serving on the front line on that day, and was caught in no-man's-land during a heavy bombardment. I was injured, and took cover in a large bomb crater and found William there. He had been badly wounded. He was an enemy, but we were also two men, human beings together, frightened and facing death, and so I treated his wounds as best I could. We talked as we waited for the shells to stop falling. He told me about you, and about his younger brother Charley.

"He knew he was dying, and he asked me to write to you, so that you would hear what he had to say at the end of his life. He was proud to have served with his friends, but was very sorry for leaving you and his brother. He asked me to tell you that he loved you both, and he hoped that you would think well of him for becoming a soldier. But he begged you to ensure that Charley did not enlist, for death feeds in this place, and no mother should have to lose two sons to this accursed war.

"I apologise for the lateness of this letter, but I was hospitalised for some time with my own wounds, and have only recently recovered enough to write to you. Mrs Burn, I might never know if you will believe this, for William and I fought on opposite sides of this conflict. But though I only knew him for a short time, I want to assure you that I stayed with him until the end, and that he died with a friend at his side. I offer my deepest sympathies for your loss. Oberleutnant Karl Ehrlichmann."

Charley was crying as he read the last few lines. Mick squeezed his hand, but Charley felt the weakness in his friend's grip and looked down to see Mick's eyes were becoming glassy and unfocused.

"That's terrible, Charley," Mick said in a slurred voice. "It's horrible."

"The first of July," Charley said, wiping his eyes with a filthy hand. "That was the first day of the Somme. He was reported missing in action the next day. Mam got the telegram to say he was missing nearly a week later. But he was already gone, Mick. Will was dead before I even enlisted."

There was no answer. Mick had passed out. He was alive, but his breathing was growing ever more ragged.

"Ah, no, Mick," Charley moaned fearfully. "Not you too."

He ground his teeth together, listening to the explosions that were mashing up no-man's-land. In amidst the dull thuds of the shelling, there was the tat-tat-tat of the German machine guns. The only way to the British lines for help was through all that. Assuming he could carry his friend that far. He shook his head in resignation. Stuffing the letter back into his pocket, he stood up, grimacing at the pain in his ankle. He looked around the dug-out. It was littered with various pieces of German kit. He and Mick were both completely coated in the grey-brown mud of the battlefield, their rifles were out in the trench somewhere, and he was missing his helmet. Mick had lost his helmet too.

Charley undid his webbing belts, throwing off anything that wasn't essential. It was all too heavy. He did the same with Mick's. He picked up two German helmets. Strapping one on Mick's head, he donned the other one, and then hauled his friend's slumped weight up on to his shoulders. As he emerged from the dug-out into the trench, the noise of the shelling grew louder. From the sounds of it, everything from no-man's-land to the furthest British trenches was taking a pounding. Machine guns hammered bullets through the smoke as the Germans tried to finish off any British troops who might still be out there.

Staggering up the ramp of snow-covered earth, he looked to the right, towards his own lines, being pulverised by the artillery barrage. Then he turned to the left and carried his friend towards the ripping sound of the machine guns in the second row of German trenches. Up above ground, the crashing, cutting sounds of war were all around him. He kept his head down and kept hobbling forward, enduring the pain of his injured ankle. He heard shouting, warning cries, harsh yells in that metallic German accent. He kept his head down and kept walking, kept hoping. He still heard the machine guns, but there were no bullets passing close to him any more. Perhaps it had worked. When he finally reached the next German trench, he was exhausted, the muscles of his ankle, legs and back burning with pain. He collapsed just short of the edge, with Mick's limp, heavy body falling next to him.

In dazed confusion, he felt rough hands grab him and drag him over the edge. For the second time that day, he fell into an enemy trench, but this time there was someone there waiting. He was winded by the impact of hitting the ground.

Struggling to breathe, he tried to roll over. He saw mud-caked boots in front of his face and raised his head to find a circle of grimy, unshaven German soldiers standing over him.

"He's dying," Charley croaked. "Do you... do you speak any English? My mate's going to die if you don't help him. Please. I know what I am to you. I'll surrender to you if it'll save him. I know what I'm asking... but... Will you help him?"

They stared down at him with eyes as cold as the frozen ground he'd just crossed, saying nothing. These men, who had every reason to hate him, looked at each other as if deciding what to do with him. Charley craned his neck to see other soldiers on a ladder above him, hauling Mick in. They were pulling forcefully on him as if he was resisting them. One of them pulled a bayonet from his belt and reached up…

“No!” Charley gasped, reaching up, but he was pushed back down by hands and boots. There was nothing he could do.

A German in an officer’s uniform crouched down next to him, tilting his head to bring his face closer to Charley’s. He looked haggard, tired; a young man with an old man’s face.

“You walked with him into the machine guns for this?” he said, gesturing at the wounded man.

The soldier on the ladder cut something free from Mick’s sleeve and Mick screamed out… then jerked free – he’d been caught on something, some wire perhaps. Charley watched as these hard-eyed men lowered his friend gently to the ground.

The officer crouching next to Charley shook his head and a smile of disbelief spread across his features. “You’re either a fool or a madman. But yes, my mad friend. Yes. We’ll help you.”

Ice Fairies

SIOBHÁN PARKINSON

Illustrated by Olwyn Whelan

Siobhán Parkinson has been writing books for children for twenty years and was Ireland's first Laureate na nÓg, Children's Laureate. Apart from being an award-winning author and illustrator, she is also a publisher and translator of children's books. When she isn't writing, she likes to cook, eat, drink, sleep, sing and learn languages. Siobhán lives in Dublin with her husband, who is a wood turner, and without her grown-up son, who does mysterious things with words in England.

Olwyn Whelan is a children's book illustrator living in Dublin with her husband and two children. She has been shortlisted twice for the Children's Books Ireland Award for children's books. Her latest book is *Spellbound*, written by Ireland's first Children's Laureate, Siobhán Parkinson.

Someone had dressed the icicles. Well, decorated them anyway, with ribbony wisps of fabric, so that it looked as if small colonies of fairies had taken up residence in the trees.

The children came rushing out of school, delighted with the snowy park. It was thigh high on the littlest ones, and had drifted deep in corners. The playground was locked, though. 'Health and safety' a hurried note flapping on the bars of the gate announced gloomily. But the children didn't really mind. All the swings and slides had grown a thick white fur, like static polar bears – only more *glistening* – and anyway the icy paths were far more inviting than playground slides.

The sky bent low and purplish over the park, but there would be light enough to play by for an hour or two yet, the biggest children informed the youngest ones, who wondered how it was that larger people always seemed to know so much: they could even tell the future, it seemed.

It was one of the very smallest children, though, who first noticed the fairies in the trees.

"Look," he said, pointing a small damp finger up into the air – and if you are an older child, which you must be if you can read this, you have probably noticed that the fingers of much younger children usually are rather damp, though there really is no very good reason why they should be, but there you go, life is full of mysteries.

"Fairies," announced the small child, quite matter-of-factly, as if that was an interesting enough sort of discovery, but after all only to be expected when the weather turned cold. For all he knew – he never had experienced snow before – fairies were part of the package, like frost patterns on the windscreens and water you could walk on.

"Don't be silly," the older children said (practising for being grown-ups), for they had experienced snowy weather before and knew that fairies were not a weather phenomenon.

"No, wait, he's right," said a middling-sized child (who happened to be the small boy's sister, and knew he didn't say silly things – or not much). She was looking where the small boy was pointing. Brian was his name, but unfortunately he was usually referred to as Brain at school. "There really *are* fairies."

"Ice fairies," Brain – I mean Brian – explained.

Then all the children looked up into the trees, and, sure enough, remarkably, every tree, it appeared, was populated by ice fairies. Not even the eldest children, and one or two of them might have been as old as ten – which is double digits, and thus in a different category entirely – not even they could deny that there were indeed fairies in the trees in the park where they played every afternoon and where a fairy had never before been encountered. This was very strange. It might even be a matter that would eventually have to be referred to the grown-ups.

There was a hurried consultation among the double-digit children. The question was this: should they climb up on each other's shoulders and make a human pyramid so the top child could reach the fairies? Bartholomew was for the human pyramid. He'd seen it in books, and he'd always wanted to do it, but he'd never been able to get his friends to cooperate. Here was the perfect opportunity. But Leonora (Brain's sister) said, very sensibly for a child still only in the single digits, that a human pyramid was a dangerous enough prospect in good weather, but could only end in broken noses and sprained ankles at *the very LEAST*, she warned, in a very double-digit kind of way, "in these conditions".

"What are conditions?" asked Brain, sucking his finger.

"Weather," said Petronella. "Bad weather."

So then there was an argument about whether snow constituted bad or good weather.

"Good for sliding," said Bartholomew.

"Good for snowflakes," added Petronella, who never could be consistent.

"Good for snowballs," Brain chipped in, taking his finger out of his mouth for a brief moment.

"Bad for driving," observed Petronella, remembering which side she was supposed to be on.

"Bad for feet," said Leonora.

"*Feet?*" asked several people.

"They get cold," explained Leonora, "and wet."

"Bad for fingers," added Brain, looking at his as if he thought they might freeze up at any moment.

The children's conversation about the nature of snowy weather meandered on. But of course they weren't sitting round a table having this discussion. They were sliding up and down the park paths. They were chucking snowballs at each other and even, in one very sad case, stuffing handfuls of snow down the neck of Brain's jumper. Some of them were standing in the middle of the snow-carpeted lawn with upturned faces and open mouths, hoping it would snow right on to their tongues.

Leonora and Petronella were building an igloo behind a tree. Or at least, they were having a civilised discussion about the best way to build an igloo, which comes to much the same thing.

So busy were the children that they forgot all about the ice fairies and they did not notice how the afternoon light thickened and thickened and the purplish sky turned deep, dark grey and silently, silently, the great black cloud over the world started to flake, astonishingly, into large white butterflies and drift, drift, drift, down into the mouths of the most patient of the waiting-on-the-lawn-with-upturned-faces children, until someone, possibly Petronella, suddenly announced, as if it were the most unexpected turn of events, "It's snowing!" and the children threw their caps in the air – those who had caps, but they mostly had hoods, so it was not exactly a *storm* of caps – and whooped and cheered and danced.

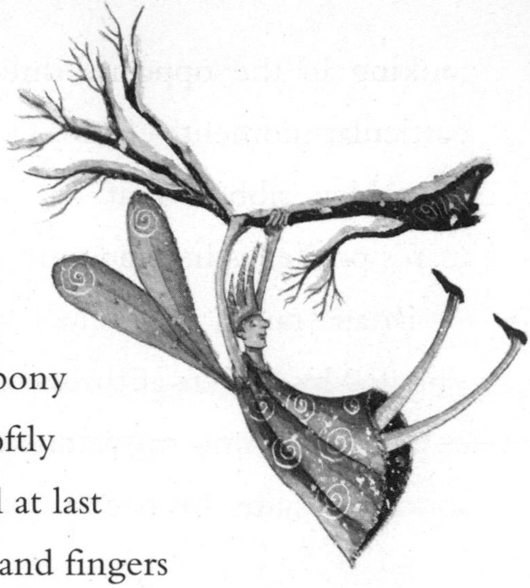

And as the snowflakes fell and fell and fell, the ice fairies hung silently in the trees, their ribbony clothes flittering softly around them, until at last the children's feet and fingers were too cold and it was time to go home to get warm, and they all turned tail and ran out of the park – all except Brian, who had stopped to say goodbye to the ice fairies. Just then the park attendant came clanging by with his closing-time bell, and nobody noticed as an old man wearing a bowler hat and a grey waistcoat shuffled off a park bench and made for the gates of the park. Nobody saw him raising his hat to the park attendant as he went through the gate – not Brian, who was still staring up at the ice fairies, not even the park attendant, who was looking in the opposite direction just at that particular moment – and nobody noticed a trail of golden ribbon that dangled from the old man's pocket as he made his way home.

Brian raised his small damp hand and waggled his fingers at the fairies. "Good night," he whispered into the dusk, and then he turned and ran off after his friends.

Discovering Bravery

Emma Brade

Illustrated by Niamh Sharkey

Competition winner **Emma Brade** is fourteen and lives in Ormskirk, Lancashire. She loves art, reading, music and writing. She has previously had some poetry published but this is the first time one of her short stories has ever made it into a book. Since Emma wants to be an author when she's older she was very delighted to have won – though also a little shocked!

Niamh Sharkey is a picture-book maker based in Dublin. Her books have won numerous awards, including the Mother Goose Award and the CBI/Bisto Book of the Year Award. Her books have also been translated into over twenty languages. Niamh was Ireland's second Children's Laureate.

"Be brave for me. I know you can do it. You just have to believe, that's all."

Ruka opened her eyes. She hung on to her brother's words, just in case they grew wings and fluttered away from her memory. As she lay in bed, she imagined they were written on the ceiling; stuffed inside the blanket that kept her warm; whispered by the chilly, morning wind. "Be brave for me. I know you can do it."

It had been almost a year since Rowan Brown had disappeared. To Ruka, he was more than an older brother; he was her best friend and her only ally. She could still remember his smiling face, the stories he would tell her when she was bored and the warm hugs he would give her whenever she cried. But one day, he went out hunting in the woods and never came back. The whole village had tried looking for him, but he was nowhere to be found.

Ruka sighed and rolled over, away from the sunlight that was streaming through the crack in the curtains. Maybe she could have just five more minutes of sleep…

"Ruka? Are you up yet?" her mother's voice called softly through the door. When there was no reply, even more light flooded into the room and a gentle hand shook the girl fully awake.

"Come on now Ruka," her mother smiled. "Today's an important day!"

Of course, Ruka remembered. Today was extremely important. Today, every ten-year-old child in the village would finally be allowed to show off their magical powers, so that they could begin training as young sorcerers. There was just one problem. Ruka didn't seem to have any magic. She was the only person her age without powers. Every day she had lived with nasty smiles and snotty remarks. How could she possibly face the other children again knowing that she was…different?

"Be brave for me."

Remembering those words one last time, Ruka swam her way up from the sea of sleep and allowed her mother to help her get ready.

A cold wind bit the cloaks of the children as they waited for their names to be called. The season was still young, so the final leaves had not yet drifted to the ground. Foreheads were creased.

Stomachs were knotted. Tension filled the air.

A group of noble sorcerers watched over the exam, frantically making notes as each pupil stepped into the centre of the courtyard and presented the magic they had learnt so far. Tiny explosions filled the area with colour, a small patch of flowers appeared in mid-air, twigs and rocks floated all by themselves and many more wondrous spells and charms were examined. But then, it was Ruka's turn.

"Ruka Brown!" one of the sorcerers chirped. A few snickers washed across the crowd as she stepped forward. The boys nudged each other and the girls began giggling. All Ruka wanted to do was crawl back into bed and let the covers swallow her up.

"Now dear," the sorcerer forced a smile before turning a page in his notebook. "Show us what you can do."

For a moment, Ruka just stood there in the empty space with the icy breeze stinging her hot cheeks. She didn't know what to do. There was nothing she could do. But she had to try.

She took a deep breath and closed her eyes. Placing one foot forward, she thrust her arms out in front of her. Hoping that nobody would notice she was shaking, she spread out her fingers and searched deep inside her heart for something, anything, which would create a magic spell. Suddenly, Ruka felt a tingling in her hands. A wave of excitement flowed through her. Was this it? The tingling got stronger and for the first time in her life, Ruka felt that she could be just like everyone else. She could learn all of these amazing spells and charms alongside other young sorcerers - all of them would become her friends - and she would never be teased for being weak or powerless again. All she had to do was concentrate.

A chill bloomed in the tips of her fingers. "It must be magic," she whispered. "It has to be!"

Ruka could feel this new strength flowing through her. Any minute now something incredible would happen! With all her heart, she pushed forward; every thought filled with new hope. Ruka gasped and opened her eyes!

Nothing. Not one ounce of magic.

She glanced at the examiner sorcerers. Some were shaking their heads, others were frowning. All of them were disappointed.

Ruka felt like a stone had been dropped into her stomach. The strength she had felt only moments ago had vanished. She didn't need anyone to tell her that she had failed.

A voice called out from the crowd of other ten-year-olds. "Wow, what a loser!" It was one of the meaner boys, laughing at her. The others followed suit and Ruka knew her face was going redder by the second. Aphra, a tall girl with a long nose swaggered over and jabbed her in the back. "Why can't you use magic, Loser Brown?" she grinned.

"I…I…" Tears began to prick Ruka's eyes. She longed for Rowan to come and save her.

Why did he have to disappear? Why couldn't he be here for her, telling all these horrible people to stop picking on his little sister?

Some of the examiners had finally started to calm everyone down, but this still wasn't enough. By now, Ruka was sobbing into her scarf. She wasn't brave. She wasn't strong. She wasn't anything. One of the sorcerers put his hand on her shoulder comfortingly. She shrugged it off. She wanted to run far away from this place. And so - with the wind howling and her cloak flowing like a faded blue river behind her - that is exactly what Ruka did.

It wasn't long before her legs were aching and her lungs were gasping for air. Gritting her teeth, Ruka tried to ignore how tired she was getting and kept running. Eventually huge trees – spindly and almost bare now that it was near winter - swallowed her surroundings and she finally allowed herself to stop for a moment.

She slumped to the ground and buried her

face in her mittens. What would she tell her parents? That she was a failure? Desperate to avoid disappointing them, she had managed to hide her weakness for all these years but this time she couldn't escape. Rowan had always been top of the class when it came to magic, but he had never boasted about it. He was the perfect student; something Ruka now felt she could never be.

A twig snapped. All of the despair in Ruka's heart was suddenly replaced with fear. The fact that she was sat unarmed in a vast, gloomy forest made her shiver. Only the bravest of hunters dared enter places like this. There were always those who didn't return - and Rowan was one of them. Young children were told never to leave their village because 'bad things' would happen. This was the furthest away from home Ruka had ever been and worst of all… she was alone.

She timidly raised her head, her eyes wide with fright as she scanned her surroundings. At first it seemed like nothing was there but then, she saw them.

A pair of golden, lamp-like eyes were staring at her from the early morning shadows. They gleamed as the light danced through the tree branches, yet the pupils were so sunless they seemed to cast the entire forest into darkness.

Ruka swallowed a scream and pressed her back into the bark of the tree. She couldn't move.

Slowly, a paw emerged from the shade, followed by a long snout, ears that were stood to attention and an elegant, swishing tail. A wolf.

As it gradually came closer, Ruka could feel herself shaking. This was it. She was going to be eaten. Desperately, she tried to remain calm in the hope that the wolf would lose interest and go away but its eyes were fixed on hers, its gaze as pointed as knives. By now, Ruka was trembling all over. She turned away, not wanting to see the fangs that were about to gobble her up. Then she felt something like damp sandpaper on her cheek and every bone in her body went cold.

Ruka turned to face the wolf. It had just licked her.

She blinked a few times and stared at this now innocent-looking creature. Its thick snout and stocky build seemed to suggest it was male. He looked at her as if he was expecting something, his tail thumping the ground. When Ruka didn't move, the wolf decided to take matters into his own hands.

He circled around a few times, almost as if he was chasing his tail. Ruka watched, still feeling a little nervous. *What is he doing?* she thought to herself. *All the old stories Grandmother told me were about wolves who were evil and greedy. But this one looks just like a nice pet dog.*

The wolf paused abruptly with his nose pointed to the sky. To begin with, nothing happened. But then, with a shudder, blue sparks appeared in the air just above the wolf's muzzle. They flitted about for a moment before gently fusing themselves into a snowflake that rested on the tip of his snout. It was beautiful, like silver crystal that sparkled with glittery wonder.

Ruka couldn't hide her amazement. Feeling a little more relaxed, she clapped at this strange sight. This seemed to please the wolf, a new energy awoke inside him and he began to dash about in excitement, leaving the snowflake to fall to the ground. This made Ruka giggle.

"Not so scary now, are you, Mr Wolf?" She grinned. The wolf began to pull on her cloak; he seemed to want her to follow him. Ruka laughed and got to her feet. Before she knew it, he was dashing off into the distance. No longer feeling any danger, she decided to follow.

The wolf yapped and barked happily as Ruka ran to keep up with him. This time, the breathlessness was different. It was filled with joy instead of sadness. There were no tears to blur her vision. She didn't care where she was going any more. All that mattered was that she was having fun, as was this mysterious beast that occasionally seemed to look back at her with the closest thing to a smile that a wolf could wear.

At that moment, with a majestic sweep, the wolf's tail began to dip towards the ground as he ran. Ruka watched in awe as his fur appeared to glow white. All of a sudden a sea of light washed over the forest and with a gasp, Ruka realised that she was running on the pearl-like surface of snow. It was the perfect kind; light and fluffy like one of her mother's desserts but also sturdy enough to build the greatest of snowmen.

The wolf's tail had become a sort of wand and every time it swished through the air, a small blizzard covered the once bleak forest. Ruka laughed – the sound like sleigh bells – as she danced and twirled in this wintery heaven. As a ray of sunlight pierced through the trees, the wolf ran in a circle around her and Ruka put her hands to her head, to feel tiny diamonds and delicate silvery flowers settling in her short, brown hair. It was like wearing a beautiful crown.

Ruka blushed slightly as the wolf lowered his head in respect. In that moment, she became the Queen of this small wonderland.

It wasn't long before the excitement began again. With a flick of the wolf's nose and more swishes of his tail, mounds of snow began to gather all around Ruka. They grew arms, legs and even faces. Giant people, each of them glowing as the winter sun shone down on them, rose up from the ground. Each one smiled and bowed to Ruka. One of them even shook her hand! But it didn't feel cold. Nothing in this world was cold.

The wolf still wasn't finished building this magical kingdom for Ruka. Raising his head, he howled to the clouds above. That echoing sound sent sparks of energy through Ruka's veins and she threw her head back and whooped in delight. Her heart felt electric and beat faster and faster. What new, wonderful things would be shown to her next?

In response to the wolf's call, shining shards

of ice flitted down from above. Up close, Ruka could see that they had tiny wings glittering with one thousand colours. They were fairies. Everything about them looked extremely fragile and Ruka suddenly became afraid of moving – for surely even the smallest motion could hurt them. But with a laugh, each fairy poked Ruka's nose before disappearing in a puff of blue smoke, leaving a delicious cool breeze on her cheeks.

The wolf looked up at her, obviously proud of the world he had created. This was the happiest Ruka had felt for a long time. All traces of loneliness and shame had vanished. She wished this day could last for ever. But she knew that soon, she would have to go home and tell her parents about the test. She would have to return to the place where she was bullied every day, the place where she wasn't important or special or the ruler of an entire world, however small.

Feeling a sudden rush of love, Ruka knelt down and threw her arms around the wolf, burying her face in his fur. It was soft and warm and she could feel the steady tick of his pulse next to her ear. The wolf's tail wrapped around her and he nuzzled her shoulder with his nose.

"Thank you," Ruka whispered, her voice wobbling slightly. The wolf gave a little whine in response and playfully licked her cheek. She laughed and hugged her new friend harder.

But then… the spell was broken.

Everything around the pair suddenly vanished. The snow, the giants and even the crown on Ruka's head.

A sound of heavy footsteps grew closer and closer. The wolf went tense and every muscle beneath his fur seemed to strain. A shadow fell over her and Ruka felt awfully small. Shaking, she turned to face… a monster.

A warty, slimy face stared down at her. Yellow eyes with black slits for pupils met her own. The skin was a murky grey colour and was covered in deep scratches. Its body was huge and covered in mud. The only clean-looking thing about its appearance was its bared teeth; gleaming white and deadly sharp. A goblin.

Ruka just managed to scramble out of the way before it struck her with its claws. With a roar of frustration, the goblin leapt at her again. Once more, Ruka threw herself to the side, dodging the monster's grasp.

Panic was flooding her thoughts. She cried out for someone to help her, but of course, nobody could hear. Only the wolf – but he seemed strangely calm. She looked down at him, searching for anything in his expression that might tell her what to do. The animal looked back at her with a determined gaze and Ruka thought she saw him nod his head. There was something strikingly familiar about the way he did so.

Be brave for me.

Those words flashed in Ruka's memory like

a bolt of lightning. Time seemed to slow down around her. With a quivering hand she brushed away the tears in her eyes and tried to steady herself as she heard a quiet voice in the back of her head saying, *I know you can do it.*

The goblin was coming closer, its claws and teeth prepared to strike. Ruka tried to ignore the sick feeling in her stomach as she reached out with her arms. She took a deep breath and closed her eyes.

There it was again. That tingling feeling. But it was only faint. Ruka's mind couldn't stop thinking about how afraid she was, about how this time she was definitely going to be eaten.

"No!" she told herself firmly. "I am strong. I am strong!"

She thought of the wolf, the way his fur had felt so warm and cosy. She thought of the joy she had felt racing him through the snow, the happiness she had felt when her little world was created.

The tingling was stronger than ever now.

No, it wasn't tingling. It was power!

As the goblin leapt forward, it cried out and Ruka (eyes still closed) did the same! As she did so, a chilling burst of power erupted from her fingertips and waves of sharp ice devoured the goblin. The monster was frozen in place.

It howled in agony, desperately trying to escape its new prison of a frozen body. But Ruka wouldn't let it. She stamped her foot on the ground and from beneath the sole of her shoe, more ice spread across the forest floor and upwards, encasing the goblin in a shimmering blue cage. For the first time in her entire life, Ruka felt strong. A laugh managed to escape from her throat, even though she had thought all her breath vanished. She had just used magic.

"I always knew you were brave," a voice from behind her said. "And I was right."

That voice… was familiar. Already Ruka knew the face that it belonged to. But she didn't want to turn around, just in case it was a dream.

If she looked at the owner of that voice, the dream would end and she would wake up in her bed, with the sun streaming through the crack in the curtains and a stone in her heart.

She felt a hand on her shoulder. She couldn't resist much longer.

"R-Rowan?" she asked timidly.

"Hello, Ruka," her brother replied. With a snap of his fingers, the goblin faded away and silence returned to the trees once more. Ruka finally turned to face him. It was all familiar. The soft brown eyes, the messy chestnut hair and the dimple in the side of his face when he smiled. There was no doubt about it any more. After a whole year, her beloved older brother was stood in front of her.

She couldn't hold it in any more. Ruka sprang into Rowan's arms and sobbed. He held her tightly as she cried; the hug that she remembered hadn't changed. And as he held her, he explained everything in his usual, gentle voice.

"There was a terrible accident, Ruka, while I was out hunting that day. I should have been gone for good. I thought it was all over for me. But I knew that couldn't be. I couldn't leave you, not forever. Then, by some miracle, a witch found me while on her travels."

"A witch?" Ruka asked, looking wary. She had heard plenty of things about witches.

"Yes, a witch," Rowan continued. "I begged her to do something, anything that would save me. She asked me what the one thing I wanted most was and I told her. I wanted to teach my little sister how to believe in her magic.

"Of course, making a deal with a witch is never easy. She used magic to keep me alive, but I was trapped in a wolf's body. I couldn't speak to you and I couldn't come near the village. I felt so lonely and I missed our family very much. I thought about you every day.

"Then, another miracle happened. You found your way to this forest. You found me.

We got to spend time together. And I got to make you see just how magic you are."

Ruka stared at her brother in amazement. Suddenly everything made sense. Rowan had been the wolf all along. He had put on that incredible show for her. And he had summoned the goblin to teach her that she did have power. With the truth finally revealed, Ruka buried her face into Rowan's chest, hugging him tightly once more.

"We can go home now, Rowan," she said happily. "We can show everyone at school what I can do! Can you imagine how surprised they will all be? Then we can tell Mother and Father your story. They will be so happy to see you!"

Rowan smiled at her, but there was a sadness in his eyes. It was like a thin layer of mist covering a dazzling lake.

"No, Ruka," he said softly. "I can't come with you."

A lump rose in Ruka's throat and a sheet of tears slid over her dark eyes.

"W-why?" she asked, her voice suddenly a squeaking whisper. As soon as the question had passed her quivering lips, shining dust began to rise from her brother's arms.

"I have to go," he said, a smile still spread across his face. "I've done what I wanted to do and now the spell must end. I can leave happy."

Rowan was glowing now, with what seemed like an entire galaxy of stars rising up from his body and towards the heavens. Something sharp tugged at Ruka's chest. Her beloved brother was slipping away from her, disappearing like thousands of grains of sand sifting through her fingers. She clawed at his coat, holding on tight, but he was fading fast.

"No! NO!" Ruka cried. Tears were streaming down her face; she couldn't let this happen.

Rowan said her name, but now even he couldn't hide the choking sound in his voice as he held back his own tears.

"I love you, little sis. I'll always love you," he

said. "But I want you to promise me something."

Ruka stopped struggling and met her brother's gaze. She nodded quietly.

"Promise me you will never forget how brave you really are, Ruka. And never, ever give up."

Ruka blinked away the tears.

"I promise," she said. Her voice had new strength. Rowan gave one last, dimpled smile and with a flash of light, his body turned into hundreds of golden stars rising into the sky. The scene almost seemed beautiful. Then, everything went quiet.

Ruka was left alone in the middle of the forest. But her heart was prepared. She knew what she had to do. With new power flowing through her, she began to retrace her steps through the trees, steady and determined. As her village and the school came back into view at last, Ruka pressed onwards. Words were whirling in her head. Familiar words but now they whirred and ticked in her brain with a new strength.

"I believe. I am brave."

The Write to Right

We opened a creative writing centre in Dublin's inner city in January 2009. We called it *Fighting Words* – a temporary name that immediately felt like a good idea. We didn't conduct extensive market research to see if it was wanted. Nor did we seek to align it with the formal education system. We took our belief in the enterprise from 'Shoeless' Joe Jackson, in *Field of Dreams*: "If you build it, they will come."

We wanted to address the absence of outlets for children and young adults in Dublin to engage with creative writing, and the lack of time allowed for it in the school curriculum. It seemed daft, in a country that prides itself in being a land of writers, that there was so little space for writing.

From the very beginning, the interest has been colossal. We host 10,000 students each year – mainly children and young adults – at creative-writing workshops and programmes. They are all free. Most of the students come with their schools, but we also host sessions outside of school time attended by a wide range of special-needs groups, as well as individual children and teenagers. Our tutors and mentors are volunteers. We have more than 400 of them.

We had our own inspiration: we'd visited *826 Valencia* in San Francisco, a creative-writing centre established by the author Dave Eggers. We'd loved what we'd seen being done there – the way little kids were invited to put pen to paper, and the way monosyllabic teenagers were persuaded to write thousands of their own words. Since that project launched, similar creative-writing centres have opened all over the world: as well as our own *Fighting Words* here in Dublin, there are centres in Milan, Stockholm, London, Barcelona, Paris, Copenhagen, Amsterdam and Sydney, with plans for ones in Belfast, Vienna and Buenos Aires. All of these creative-writing centres are linked together informally. They communicate regularly, sharing ideas and experience.

Writing is a solitary occupation – eventually. But having witnessed it again and again over the last five years, we know that if it begins as a collective exercise, as a bit of fun, then by the time the children start to write by themselves, they produce better, more confident work. They've seen what they can do, the simple things that can make a good line brilliant, and they're keen to give it a go themselves.

Quite soon after we opened, often at the suggestion of artists from other disciplines who wanted to get involved, we started to run programmes tailored towards other types of writing, including film scripts, plays, graphic novels, radio drama, journalism, songwriting and film animation. As with those we run for creative writing, the demand by children to participate is consistently staggering, and their creativity is extraordinary.

We think creative writing is an essential part of every child's education. We want to give as many children as possible the opportunity to engage with their imaginations and see what possibilities are then opened up for them. *Fighting Words* is not state-funded, and our existence is dependent on people who believe passionately in what we do – like the writers and artists who have written and illustrated these brilliant stories. We are especially grateful to a great friend of *Fighting Words*, Sarah Webb – the creative- and driving force behind this wonderful collection.

Roddy Doyle & Seán Love

All profits made from the sale of this book go to *Fighting Words*, a registered charity.